🥜 mameshiba

ENCHANTED!

stories by
james turner

art by
jorge monlongo

Table of CONTENTS

Mameshiba: Enchanted!
Stories by **James Turner** • Art by **Jorge Monlongo**

Cover Art • **Jorge Monlongo**
Graphics and Cover Design • **Fawn Lau**
Editor • **Traci N. Todd**
Original Mameshiba character creation and design • **Sukwon Kim**
Original Mameshiba art direction • **Shoko Watanabe**

Printed in Canada

Published by VIZ Media, LLC
P.O. Box 77010
San Francisco, CA 94107

10 9 8 7 6 5 4 3 2 1
First printing, September 2013

www.viz.com

PARENTAL ADVISORY
MAMESHIBA: ENCHANTED!
is rated A and is suitable for
readers of all ages.
ratings.viz.com

Meet Mameshiba!

Edamame

Cashew

Boiled Bean

White Soybean

Pistachio

Sword Bean

Cranberry Bean

AAH!

Lentil

Chili Bean

Fava Bean

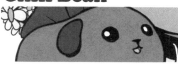

Natto

And introducing **Babyshiba!**

WHEEEE!

AIRPLANE!

mameshiba

ENCHANTED!

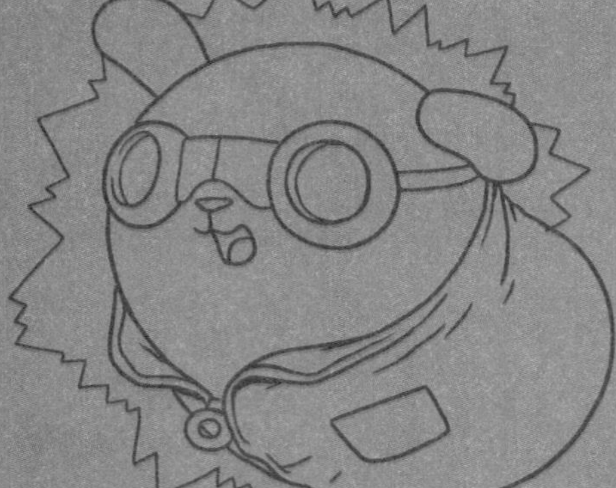

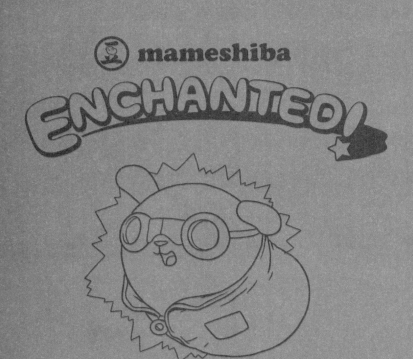

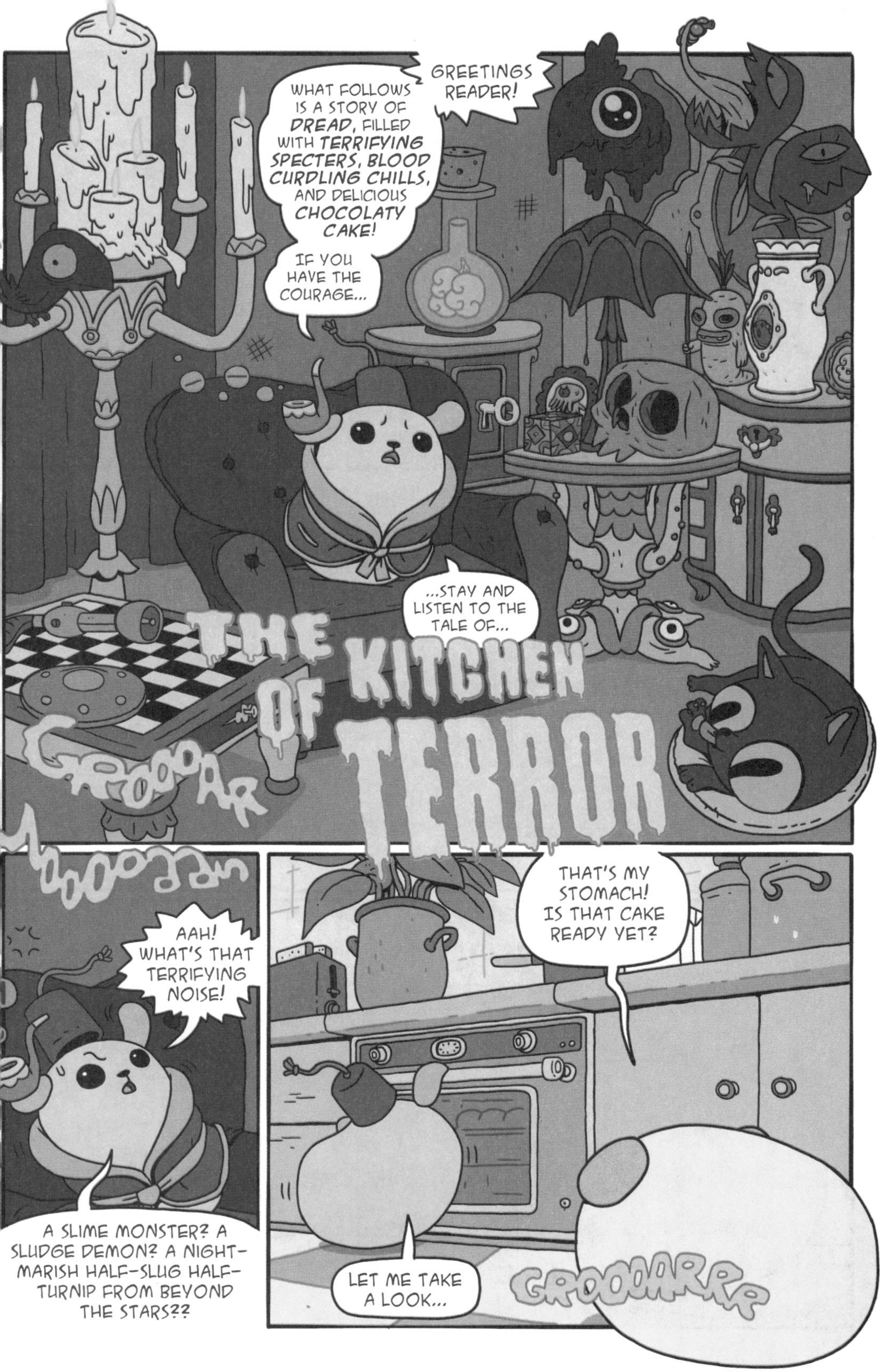
GREETINGS READER!
WHAT FOLLOWS IS A STORY OF DREAD, FILLED WITH TERRIFYING SPECTERS, BLOOD CURDLING CHILLS, AND DELICIOUS CHOCOLATY CAKE!
IF YOU HAVE THE COURAGE...
...STAY AND LISTEN TO THE TALE OF...
THE KITCHEN OF TERROR
GROOOOAR
AAH! WHAT'S THAT TERRIFYING NOISE!
A SLIME MONSTER? A SLUDGE DEMON? A NIGHT-MARISH HALF-SLUG HALF-TURNIP FROM BEYOND THE STARS??
THAT'S MY STOMACH! IS THAT CAKE READY YET?
LET ME TAKE A LOOK...
GROOOARRRR

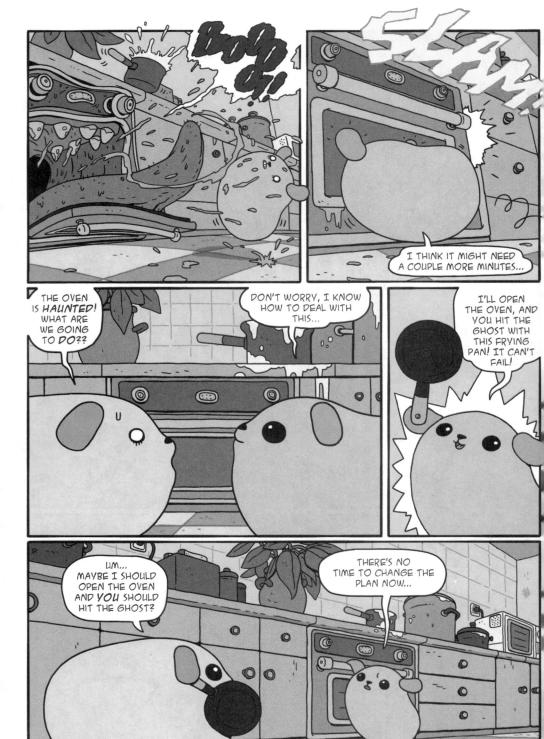

BOO!!

SLAM

I THINK IT MIGHT NEED A COUPLE MORE MINUTES...

THE OVEN IS *HAUNTED!* WHAT ARE WE GOING TO *DO??*

DON'T WORRY, I KNOW HOW TO DEAL WITH THIS...

I'LL OPEN THE OVEN, AND YOU HIT THE GHOST WITH THIS FRYING PAN! IT CAN'T FAIL!

UM... MAYBE I SHOULD OPEN THE OVEN AND *YOU* SHOULD HIT THE GHOST?

THERE'S NO TIME TO CHANGE THE PLAN NOW...

ON THREE: ONE..TWO...

WOOOO!

HIT IT! HIT IT!

ERK! OKAY, I CAN DO THIS...

BOOM!

AAH! THE FRYING PAN IS HAUNTED TOO!

QUICK!

LET'S HIDE IN THE WASHING MACHINE!

AAAAH!!!

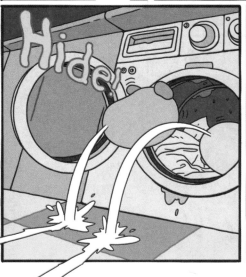

Hide!

WE SHOULD BE SAFE IN HERE!

R-REALLY?

I WOULDN'T BE SO SURE ABOUT THAT.

WHO SAID THAT??

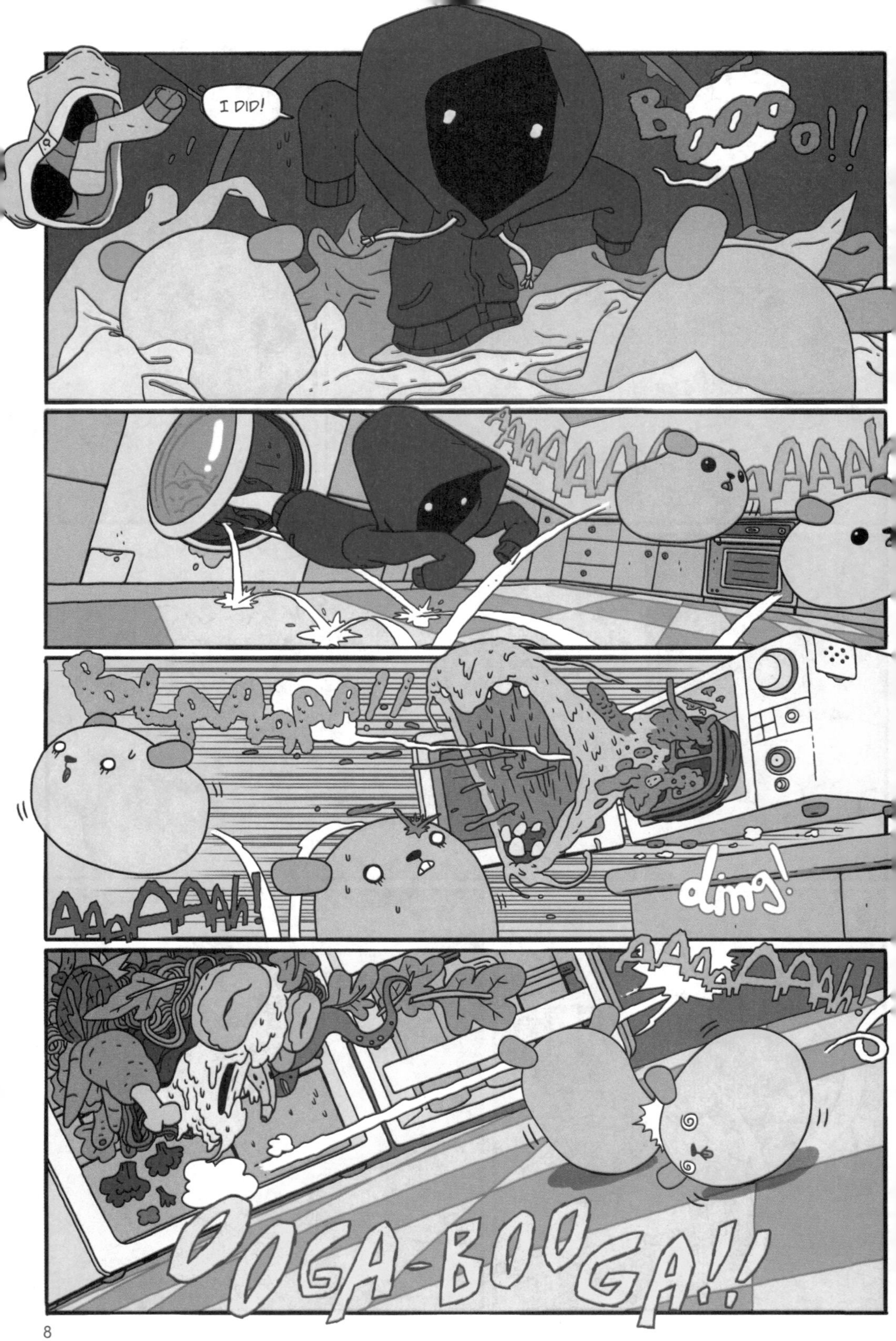
I DID!
BOOOOo!!
AAAAAAAAAAAAK
BALAAAAAAA!!
AAaAAAh!
ding!
AAAaAAAh!
OOGA-BOOGA!!

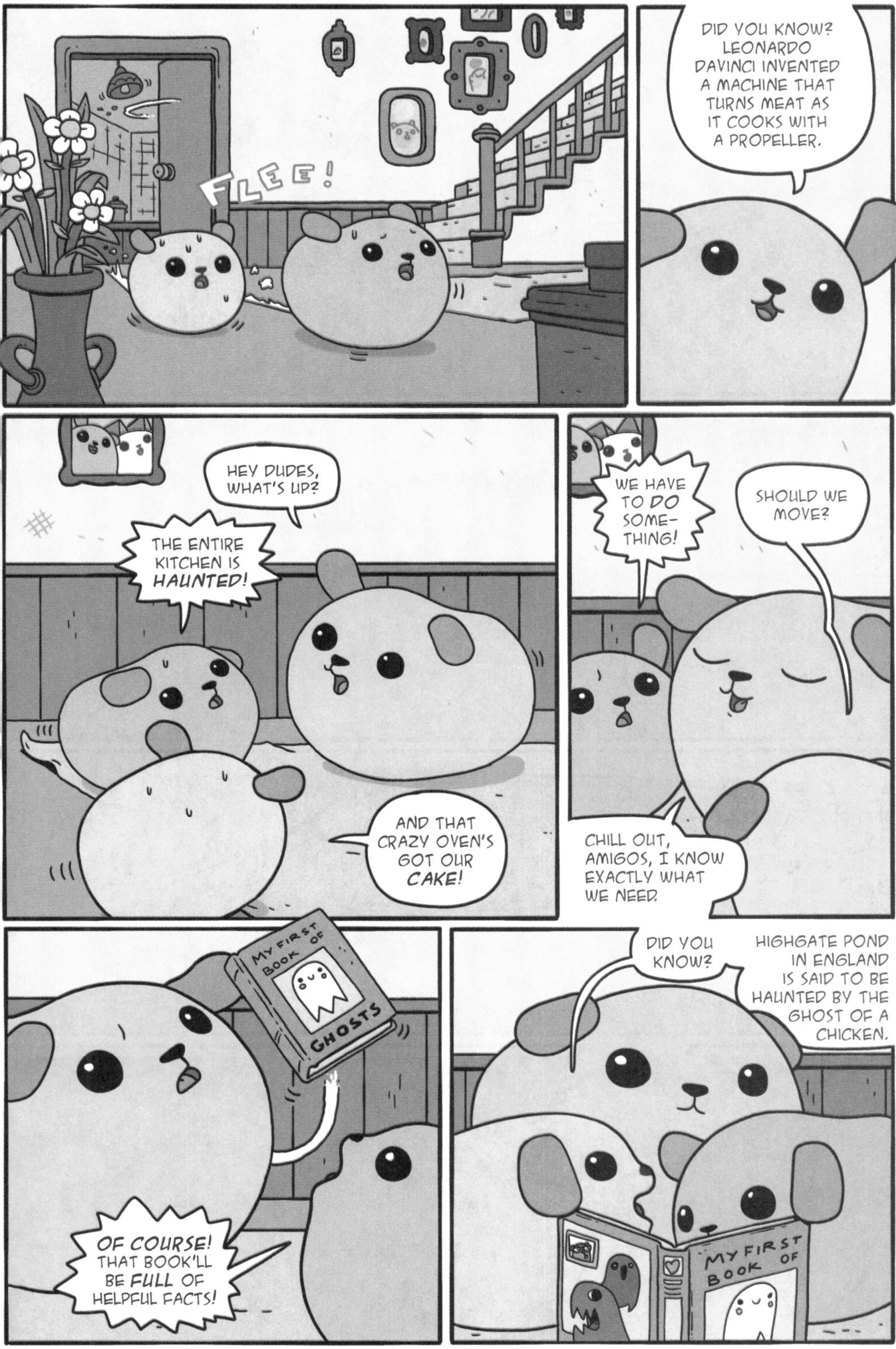
FLEE!
DID YOU KNOW? LEONARDO DAVINCI INVENTED A MACHINE THAT TURNS MEAT AS IT COOKS WITH A PROPELLER.
HEY DUDES, WHAT'S UP?
THE ENTIRE KITCHEN IS HAUNTED!
AND THAT CRAZY OVEN'S GOT OUR CAKE!
WE HAVE TO DO SOME-THING!
SHOULD WE MOVE?
CHILL OUT, AMIGOS, I KNOW EXACTLY WHAT WE NEED.
MY FIRST BOOK OF GHOSTS
OF COURSE! THAT BOOK'LL BE FULL OF HELPFUL FACTS!
DID YOU KNOW?
HIGHGATE POND IN ENGLAND IS SAID TO BE HAUNTED BY THE GHOST OF A CHICKEN.
MY FIRST BOOK OF

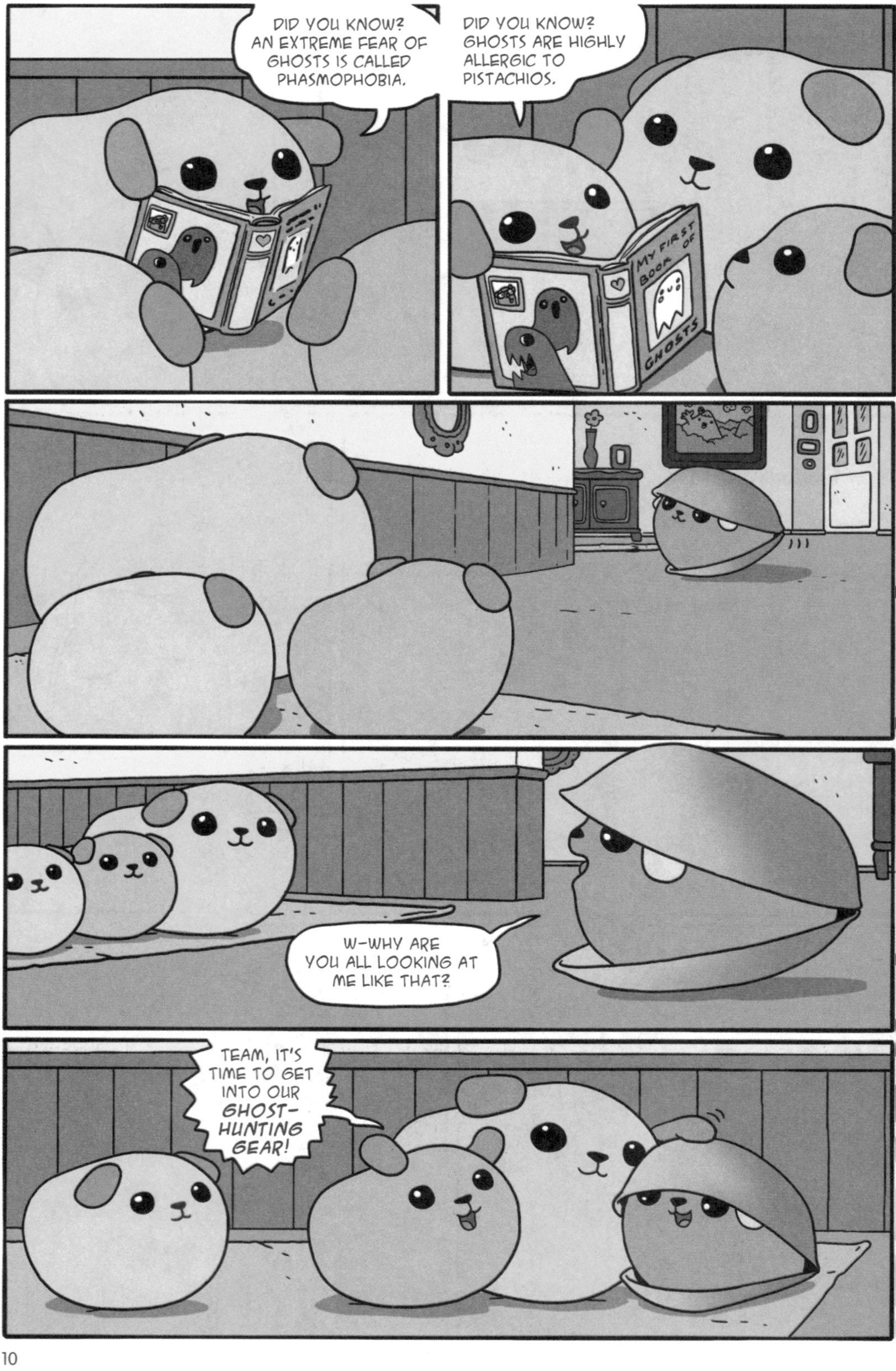
DID YOU KNOW? AN EXTREME FEAR OF GHOSTS IS CALLED PHASMOPHOBIA.
DID YOU KNOW? GHOSTS ARE HIGHLY ALLERGIC TO PISTACHIOS.
MY FIRST BOOK OF GHOSTS
W-WHY ARE YOU ALL LOOKING AT ME LIKE THAT?
TEAM, IT'S TIME TO GET INTO OUR *GHOST-HUNTING GEAR!*

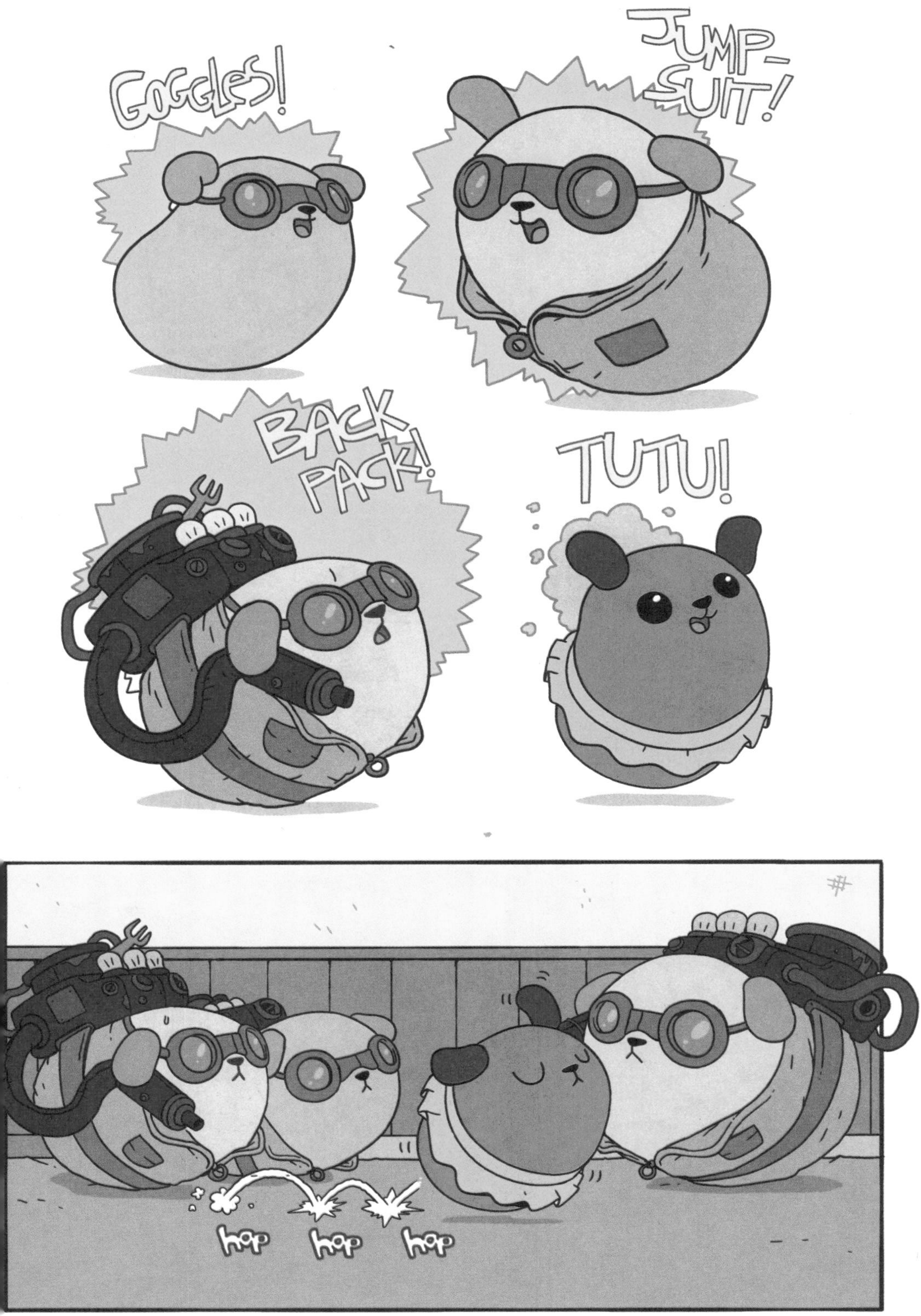
GOGGLES!
JUMP-SUIT!
BACK PACK!
TUTU!
hop hop hop

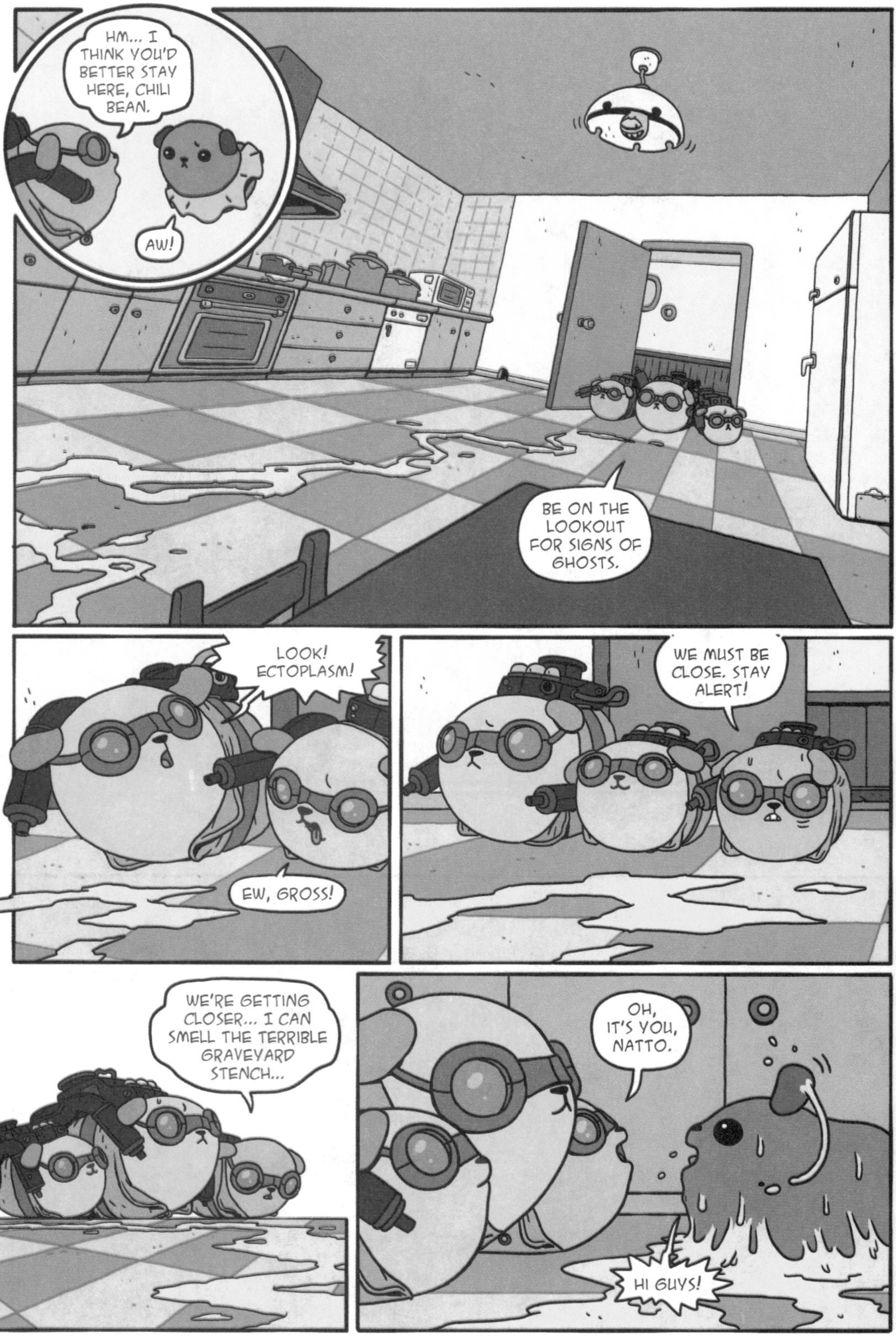
HM... I THINK YOU'D BETTER STAY HERE, CHILI BEAN.
AW!
BE ON THE LOOKOUT FOR SIGNS OF GHOSTS.
LOOK! ECTOPLASM!
EW, GROSS!
WE MUST BE CLOSE. STAY ALERT!
WE'RE GETTING CLOSER... I CAN SMELL THE TERRIBLE GRAVEYARD STENCH...
OH, IT'S YOU, NATTO.
HI GUYS!

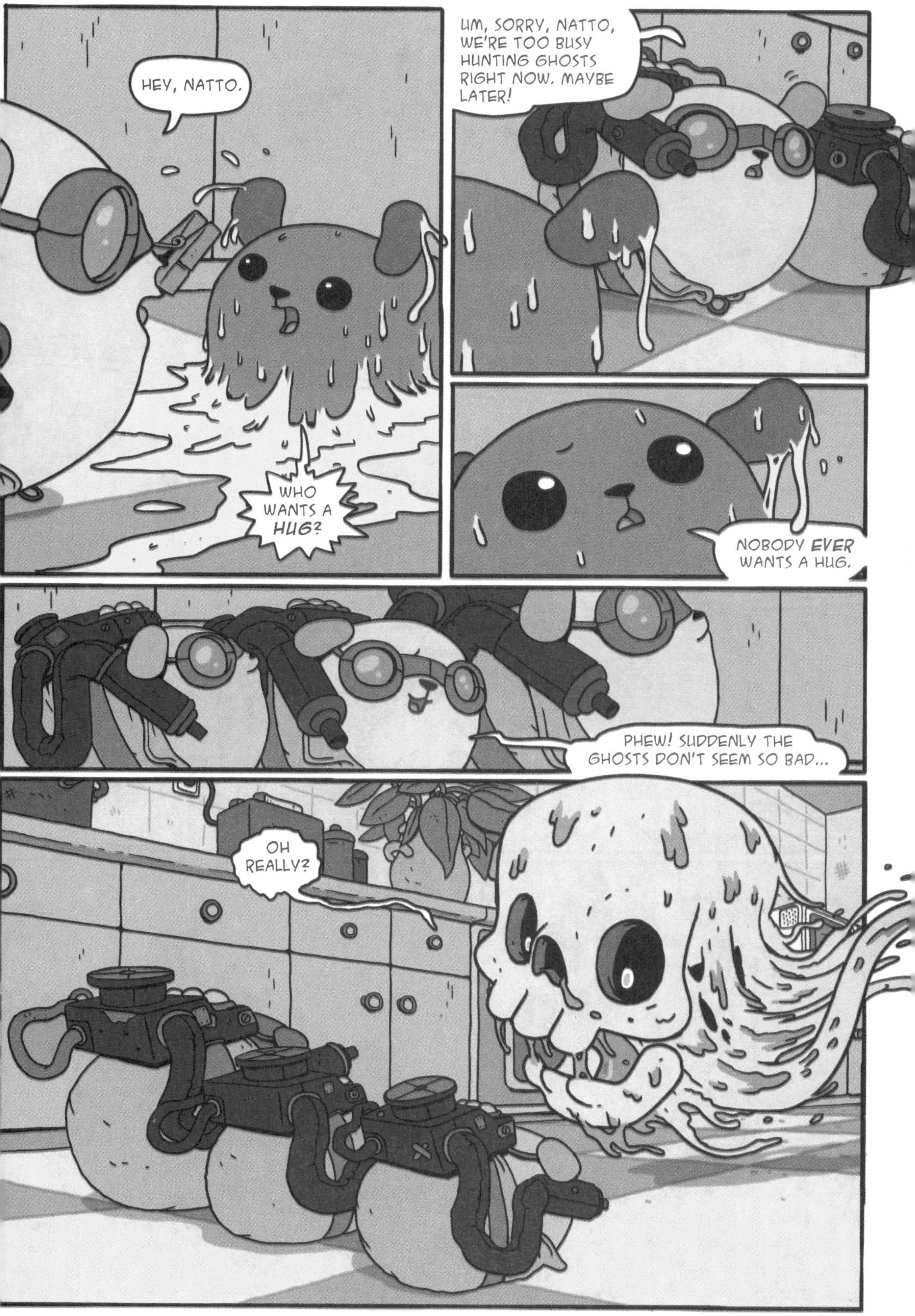
HEY, NATTO.
WHO WANTS A HUG?
UM, SORRY, NATTO, WE'RE TOO BUSY HUNTING GHOSTS RIGHT NOW. MAYBE LATER!
NOBODY EVER WANTS A HUG.
PHEW! SUDDENLY THE GHOSTS DON'T SEEM SO BAD...
OH REALLY?

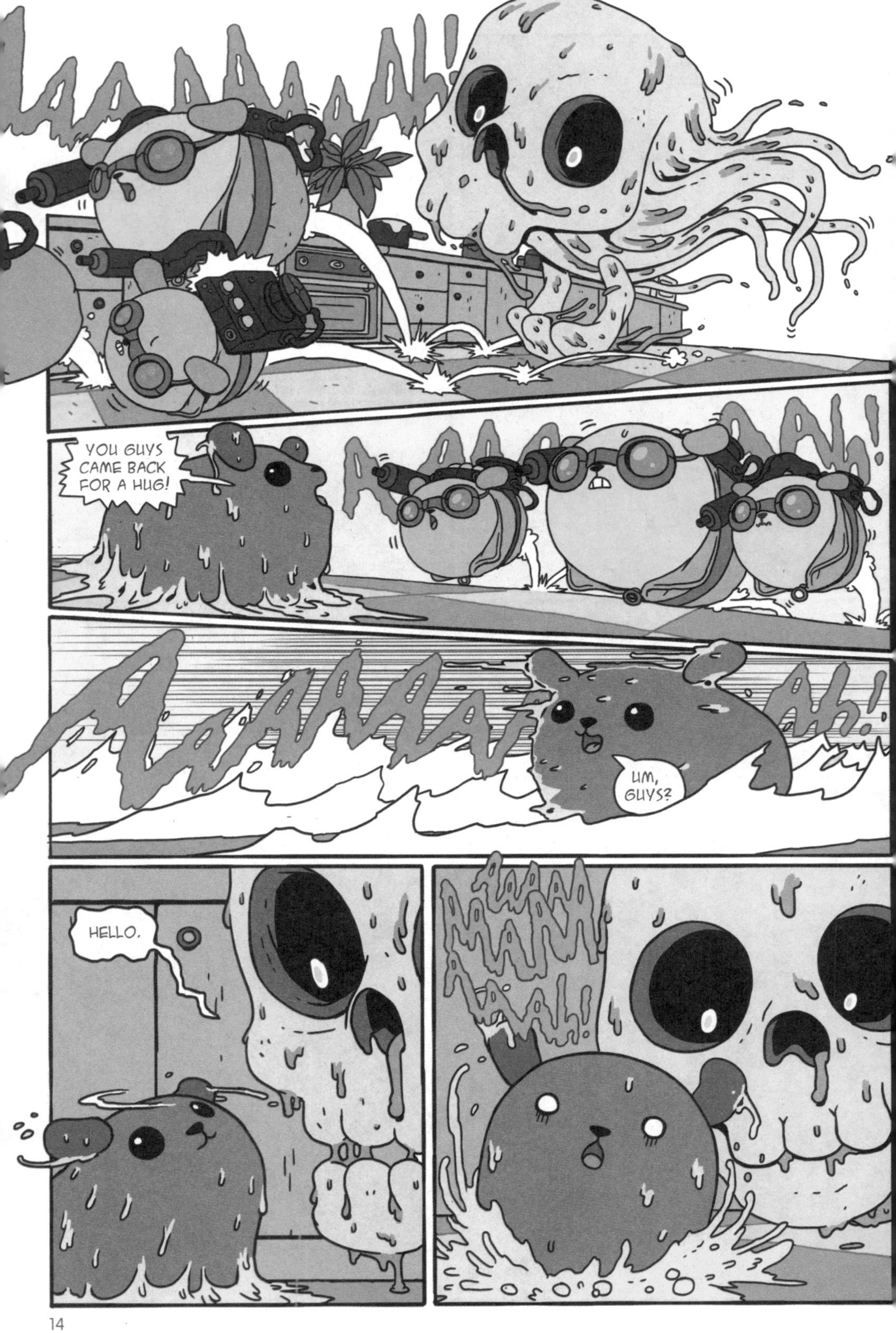
AAAAAAAH!
YOU GUYS CAME BACK FOR A HUG!
AAAAAAAAH!
AAAAAAAH!
UM, GUYS?
HELLO.
AAAAAAAAAAAH!

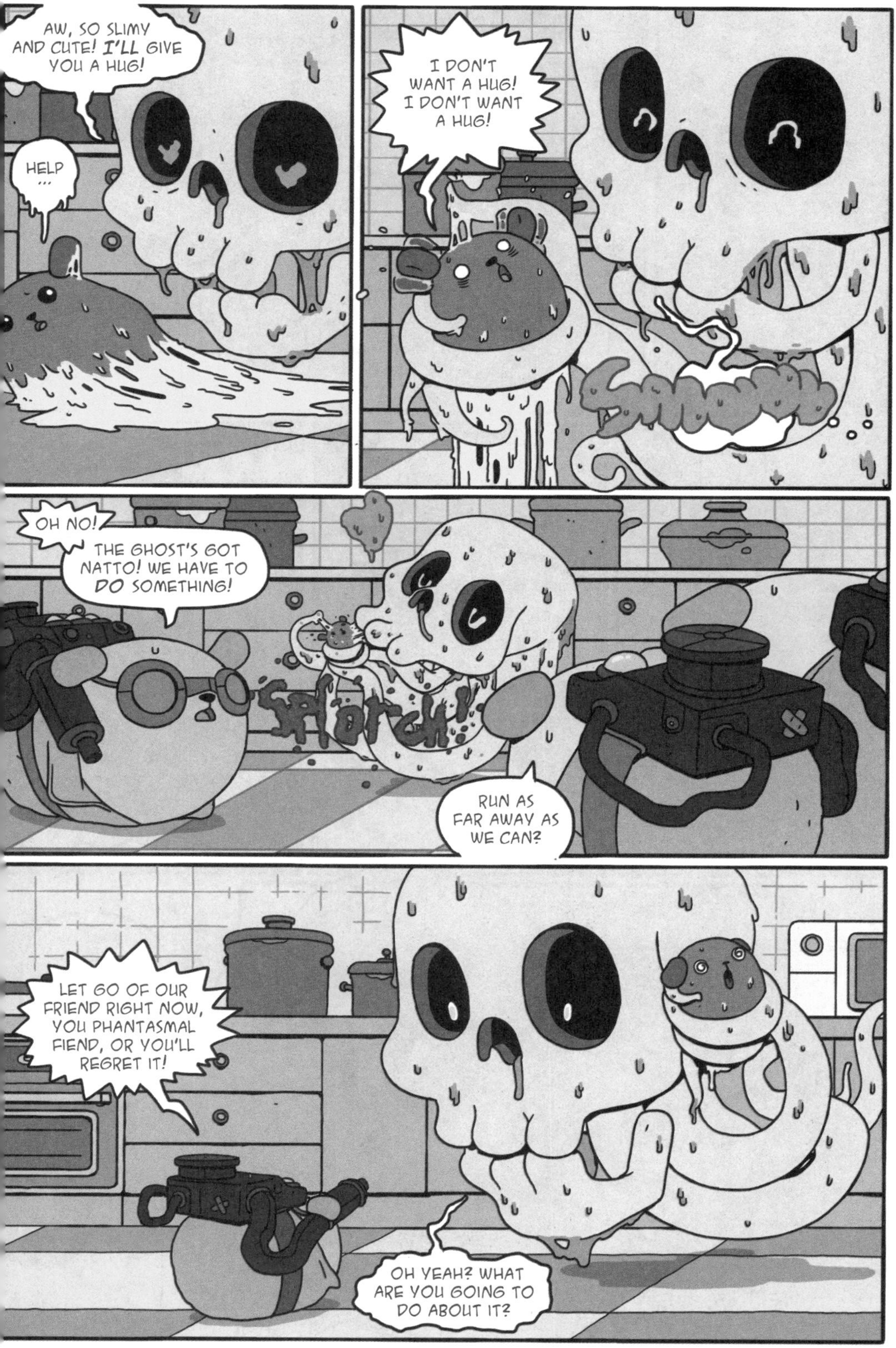
AW, SO SLIMY AND CUTE! I'LL GIVE YOU A HUG!
HELP ...
I DON'T WANT A HUG! I DON'T WANT A HUG!
SMOOCH
OH NO!
THE GHOST'S GOT NATTO! WE HAVE TO DO SOMETHING!
SPLORCH!
RUN AS FAR AWAY AS WE CAN?
LET GO OF OUR FRIEND RIGHT NOW, YOU PHANTASMAL FIEND, OR YOU'LL REGRET IT!
OH YEAH? WHAT ARE YOU GOING TO DO ABOUT IT?

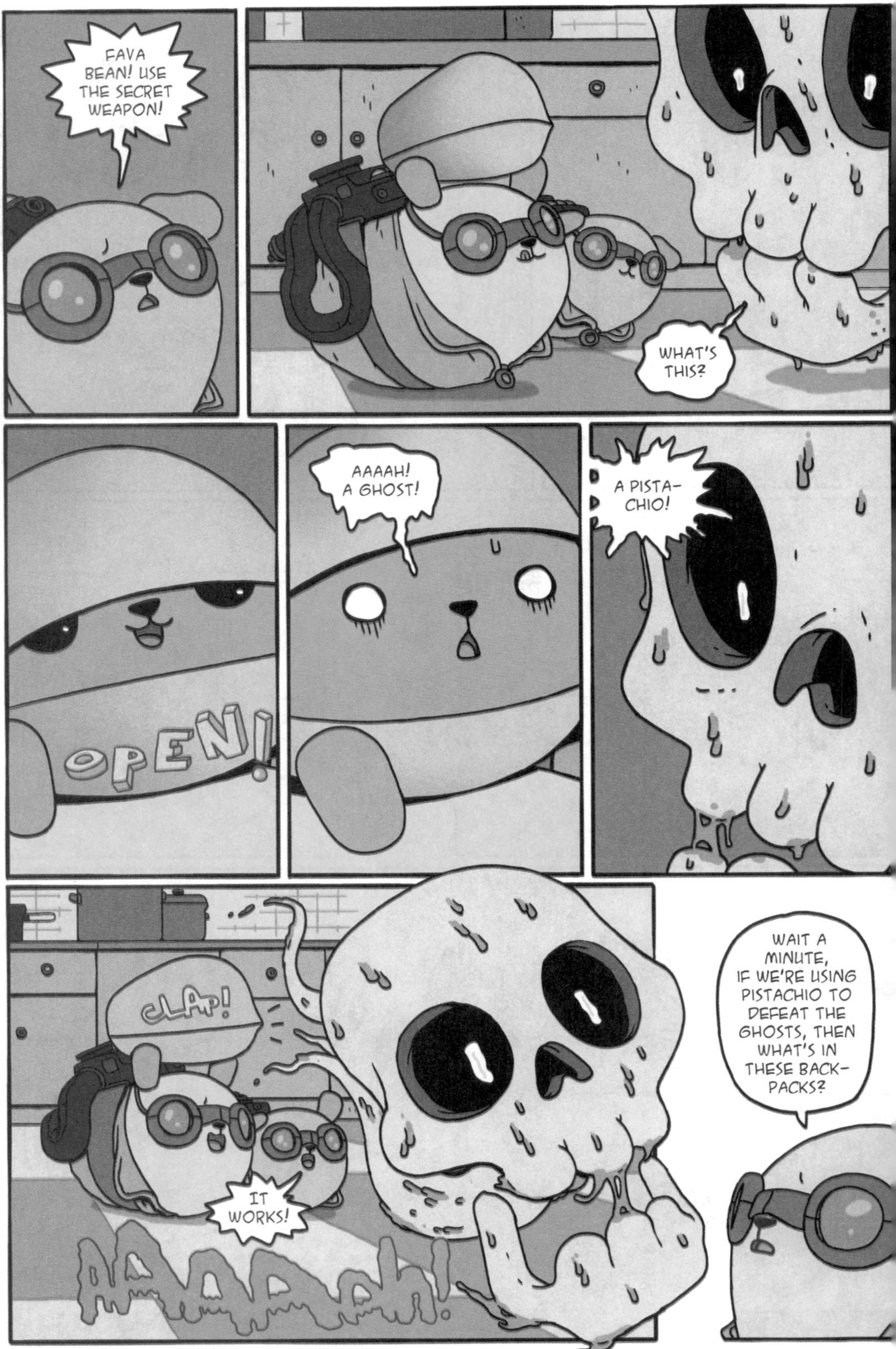

FAVA BEAN! USE THE SECRET WEAPON!
WHAT'S THIS?
OPEN!
AAAAH! A GHOST!
A PISTA-CHIO!
CLAP!
IT WORKS!
AAAAah!
WAIT A MINUTE, IF WE'RE USING PISTACHIO TO DEFEAT THE GHOSTS, THEN WHAT'S IN THESE BACK-PACKS?

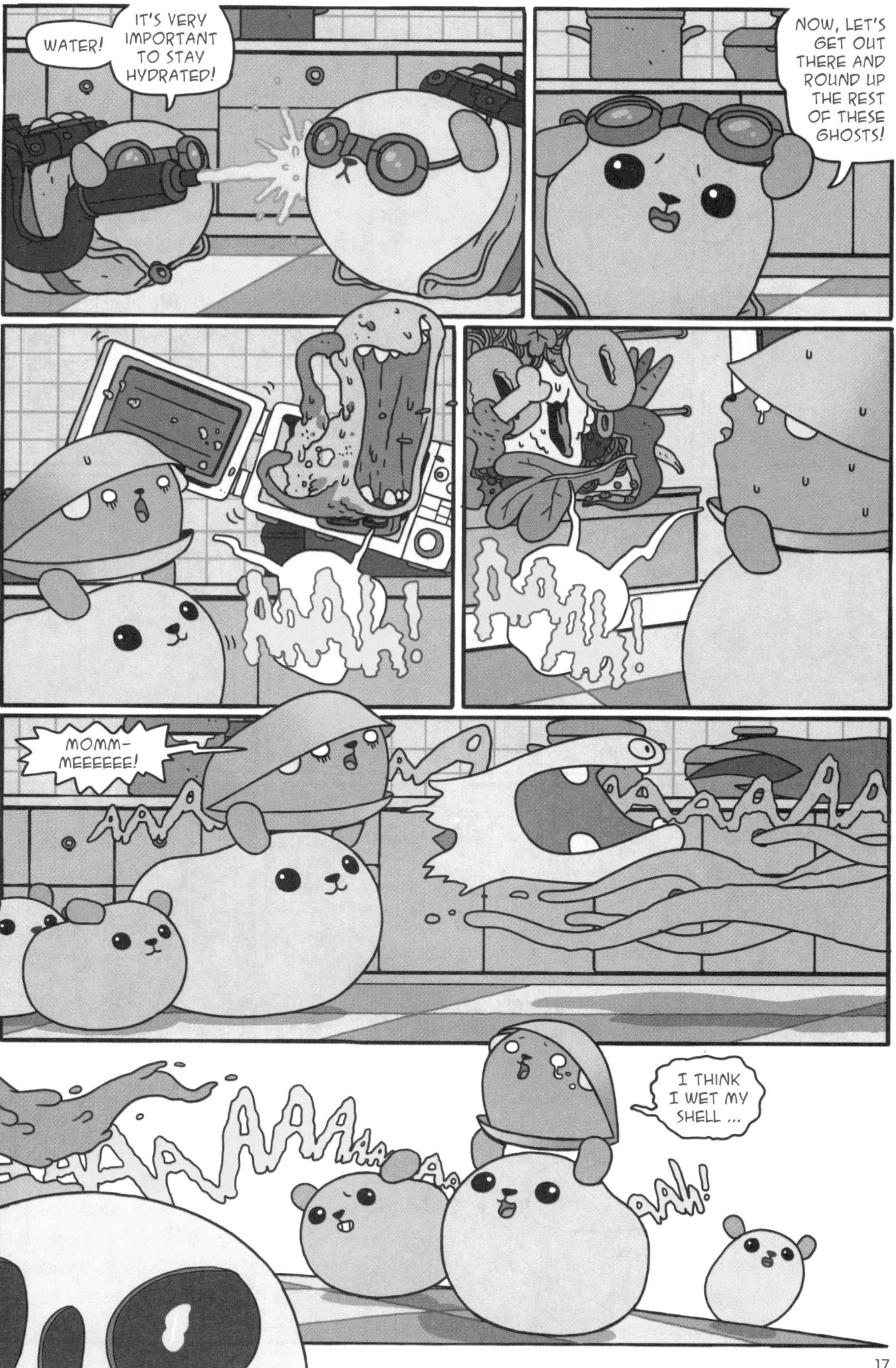
WATER!
IT'S VERY IMPORTANT TO STAY HYDRATED!
NOW, LET'S GET OUT THERE AND ROUND UP THE REST OF THESE GHOSTS!
AAAH!
AAAH!
MOMM-MEEEEEEE!
AAAAAAAA
I THINK I WET MY SHELL ...
AAAAAAAaaaaa
AAH!

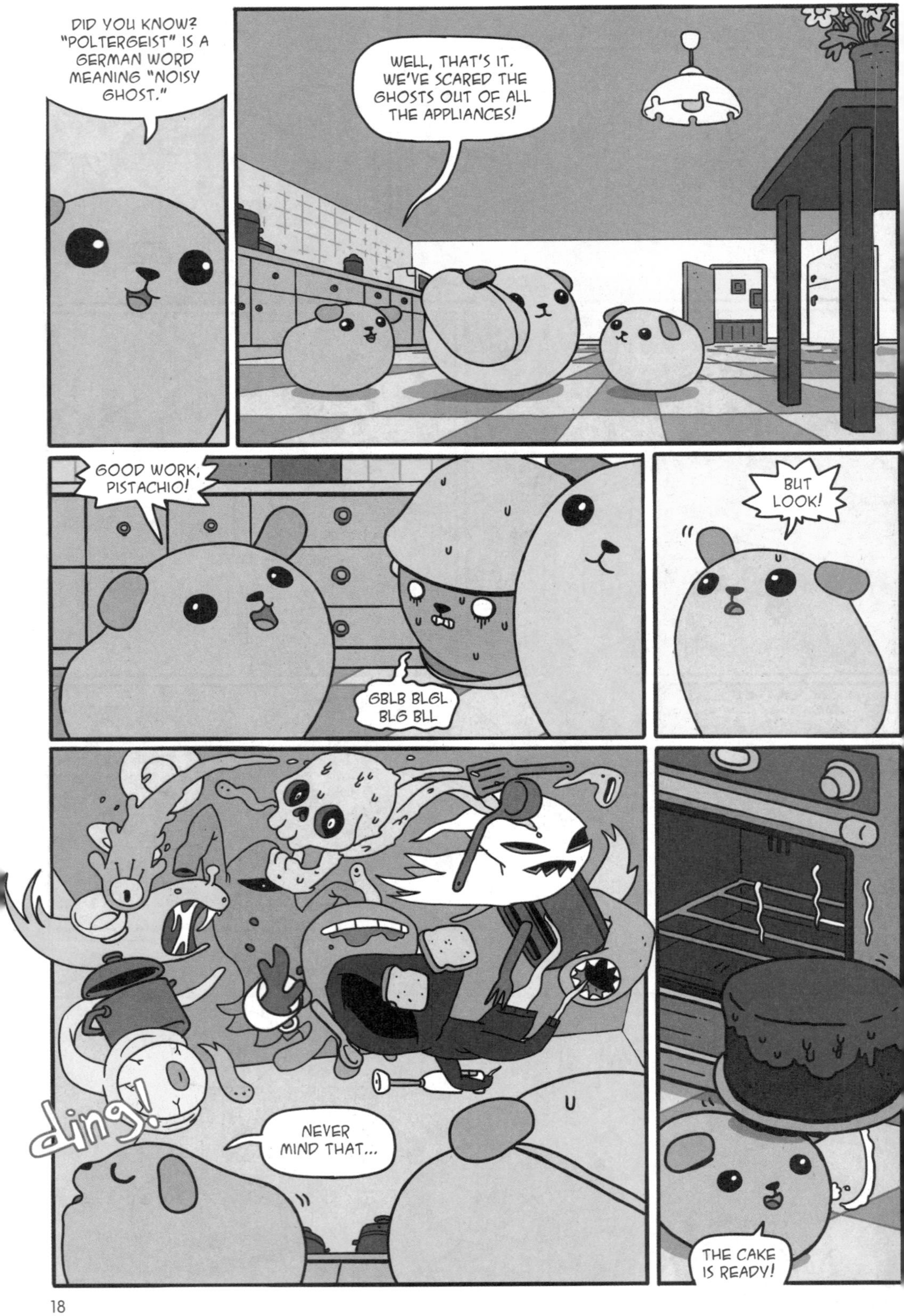

DID YOU KNOW? "POLTERGEIST" IS A GERMAN WORD MEANING "NOISY GHOST."
WELL, THAT'S IT. WE'VE SCARED THE GHOSTS OUT OF ALL THE APPLIANCES!
GOOD WORK, PISTACHIO!
GBLB BLGL BLG BLL
BUT LOOK!
ding!
NEVER MIND THAT...
THE CAKE IS READY!

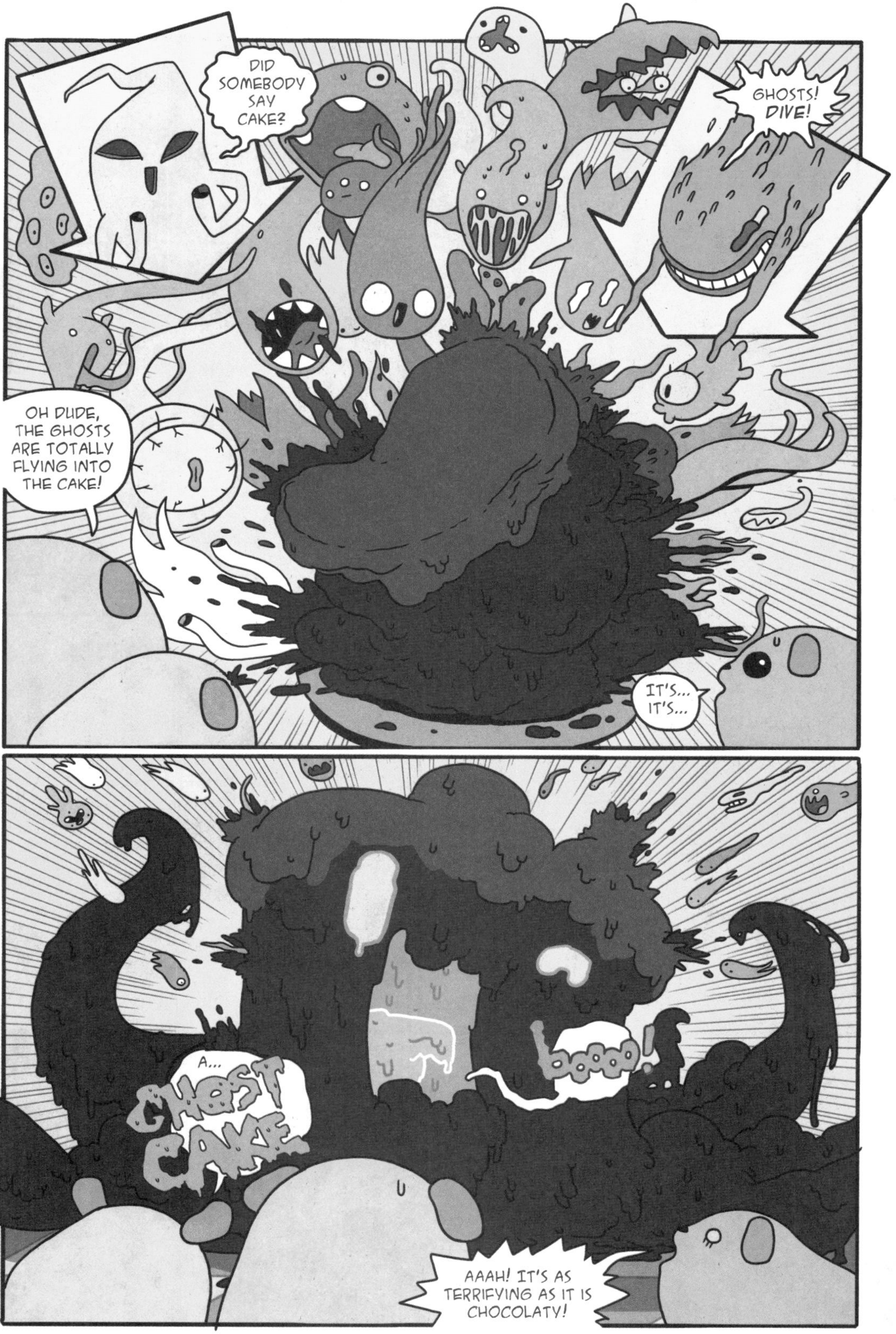
DID SOMEBODY SAY CAKE?
GHOSTS! DIVE!
OH DUDE, THE GHOSTS ARE TOTALLY FLYING INTO THE CAKE!
IT'S... IT'S...
A... GHOST CAKE
booo!
AAAH! IT'S AS TERRIFYING AS IT IS CHOCOLATY!

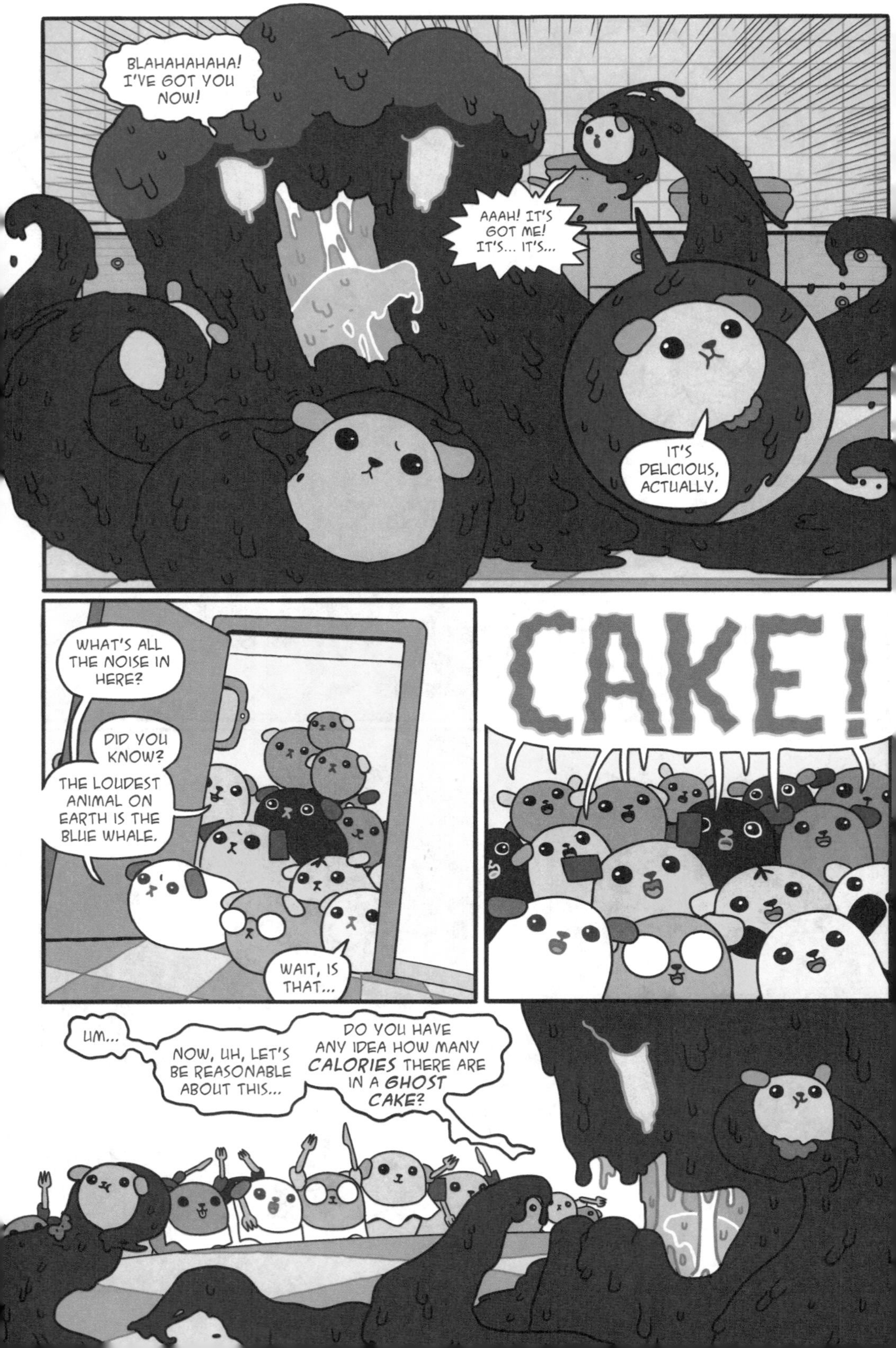
BLAHAHAHAHA! I'VE GOT YOU NOW!
AAAH! IT'S GOT ME! IT'S... IT'S...
IT'S DELICIOUS, ACTUALLY.
WHAT'S ALL THE NOISE IN HERE?
DID YOU KNOW?
THE LOUDEST ANIMAL ON EARTH IS THE BLUE WHALE.
WAIT, IS THAT...
CAKE!
UM...
NOW, UH, LET'S BE REASONABLE ABOUT THIS...
DO YOU HAVE ANY IDEA HOW MANY CALORIES THERE ARE IN A GHOST CAKE?

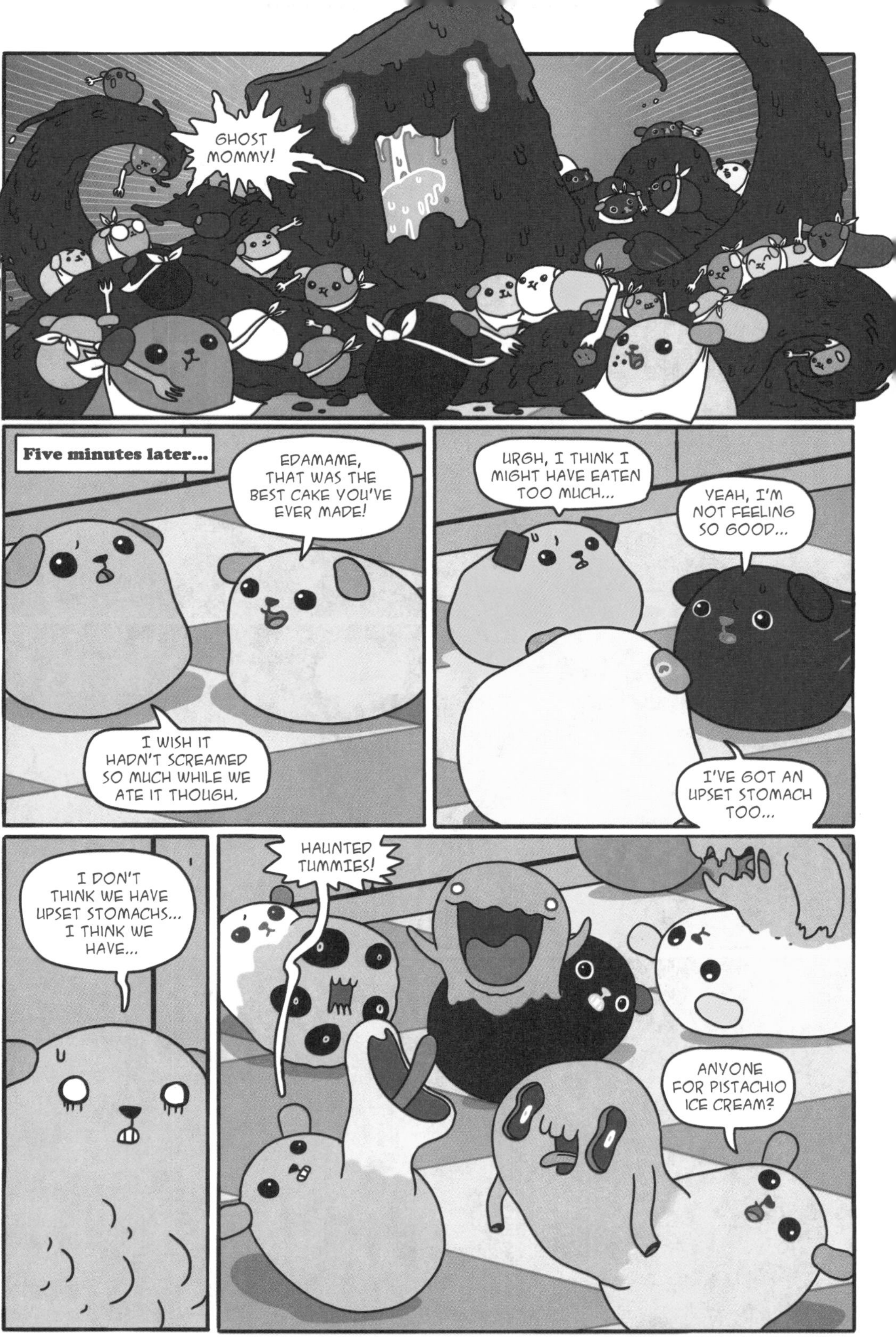
GHOST MOMMY!
Five minutes later...
EDAMAME, THAT WAS THE BEST CAKE YOU'VE EVER MADE!
I WISH IT HADN'T SCREAMED SO MUCH WHILE WE ATE IT THOUGH.
URGH, I THINK I MIGHT HAVE EATEN TOO MUCH...
YEAH, I'M NOT FEELING SO GOOD...
I'VE GOT AN UPSET STOMACH TOO...
I DON'T THINK WE HAVE UPSET STOMACHS... I THINK WE HAVE...
HAUNTED TUMMIES!
ANYONE FOR PISTACHIO ICE CREAM?

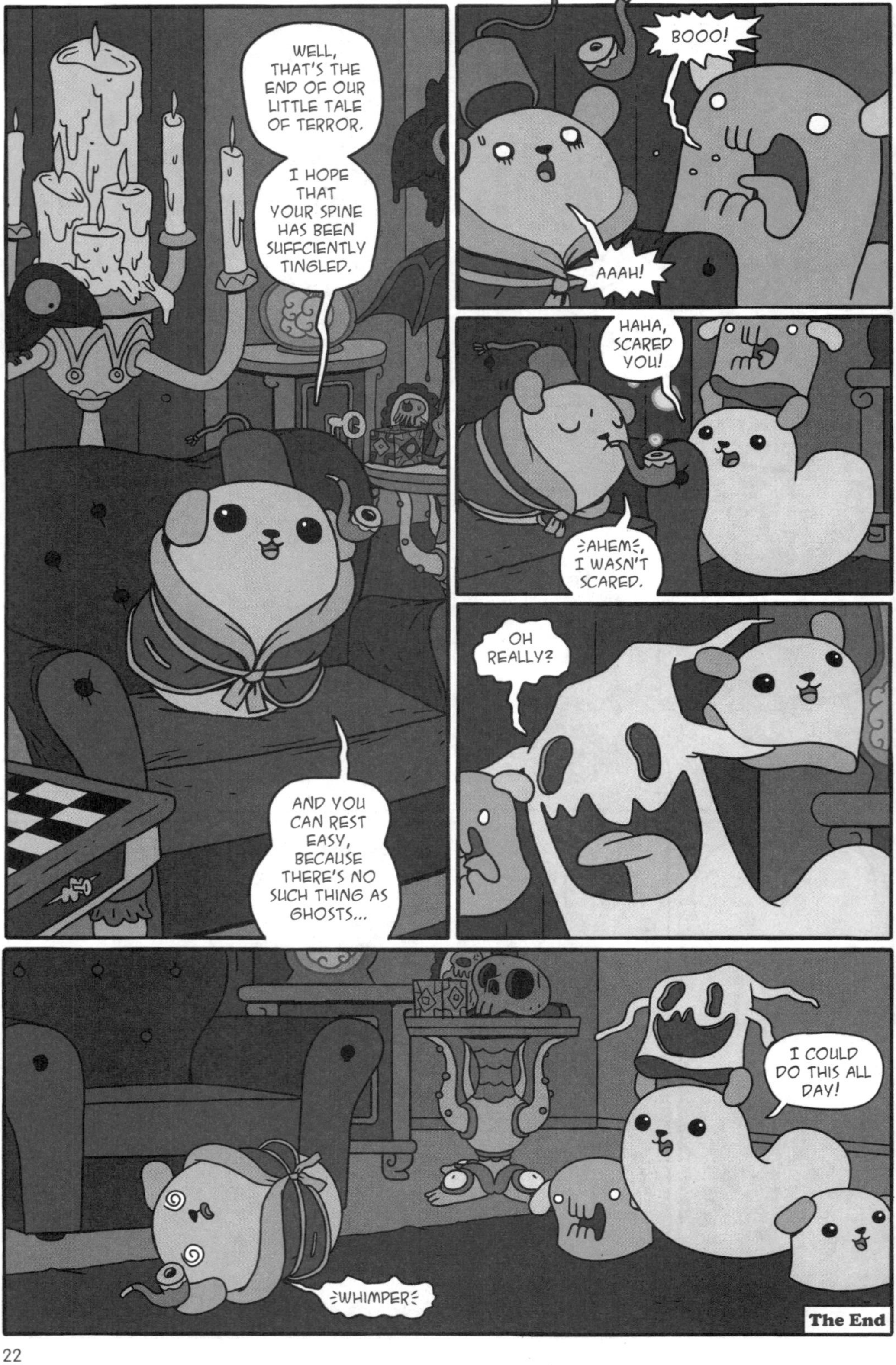
WELL, THAT'S THE END OF OUR LITTLE TALE OF TERROR.
I HOPE THAT YOUR SPINE HAS BEEN SUFFCIENTLY TINGLED.
AND YOU CAN REST EASY, BECAUSE THERE'S NO SUCH THING AS GHOSTS...
BOOO!
AAAH!
HAHA, SCARED YOU!
AHEM, I WASN'T SCARED.
OH REALLY?
I COULD DO THIS ALL DAY!
WHIMPER
The End

Cranberry Surprise

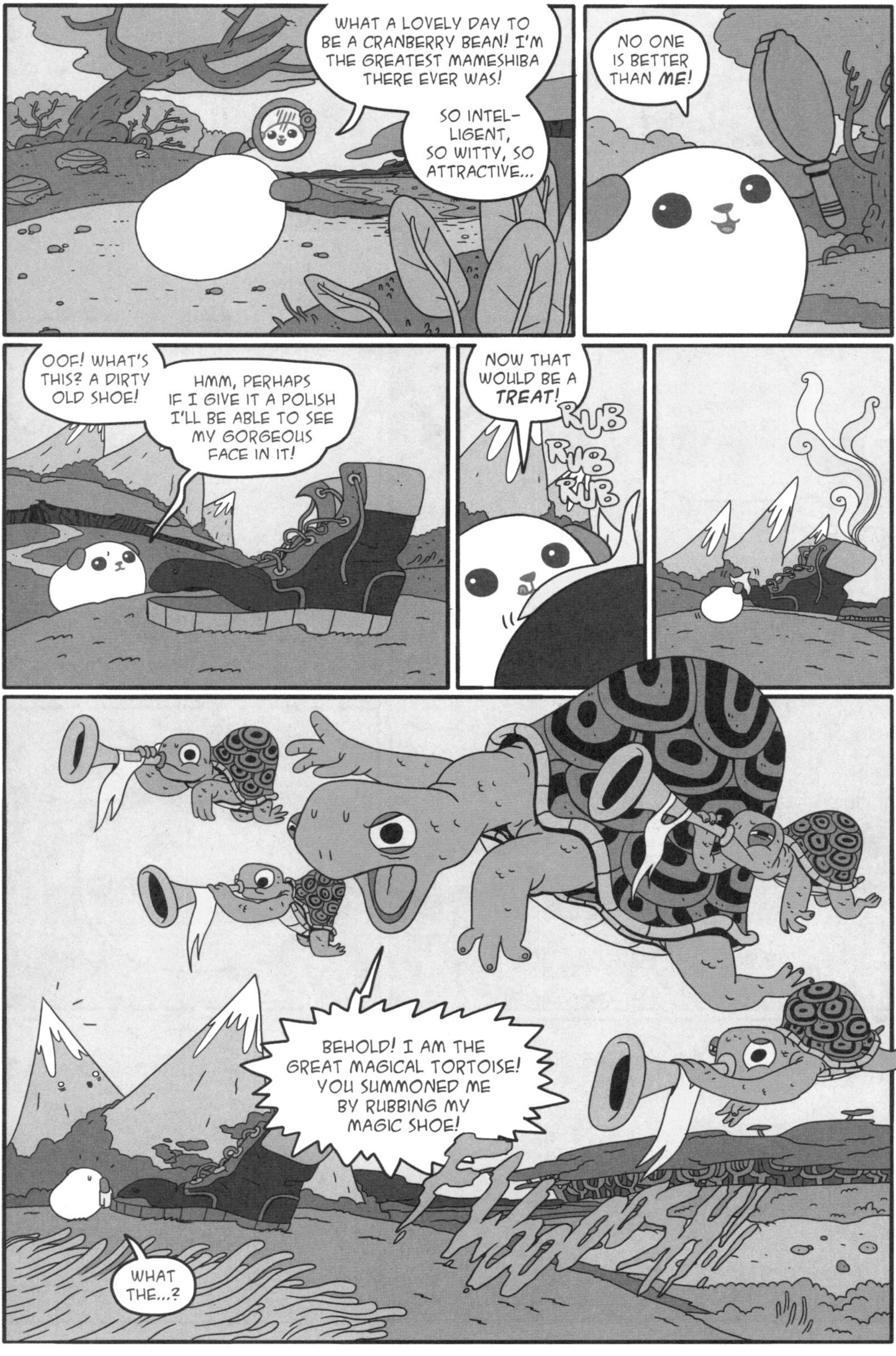

WHAT A LOVELY DAY TO BE A CRANBERRY BEAN! I'M THE GREATEST MAMESHIBA THERE EVER WAS!
SO INTEL-LIGENT, SO WITTY, SO ATTRACTIVE...
NO ONE IS BETTER THAN ME!
OOF! WHAT'S THIS? A DIRTY OLD SHOE!
HMM, PERHAPS IF I GIVE IT A POLISH I'LL BE ABLE TO SEE MY GORGEOUS FACE IN IT!
NOW THAT WOULD BE A TREAT!
RUB
RUB
RUB
BEHOLD! I AM THE GREAT MAGICAL TORTOISE! YOU SUMMONED ME BY RUBBING MY MAGIC SHOE!
WHAT THE...?

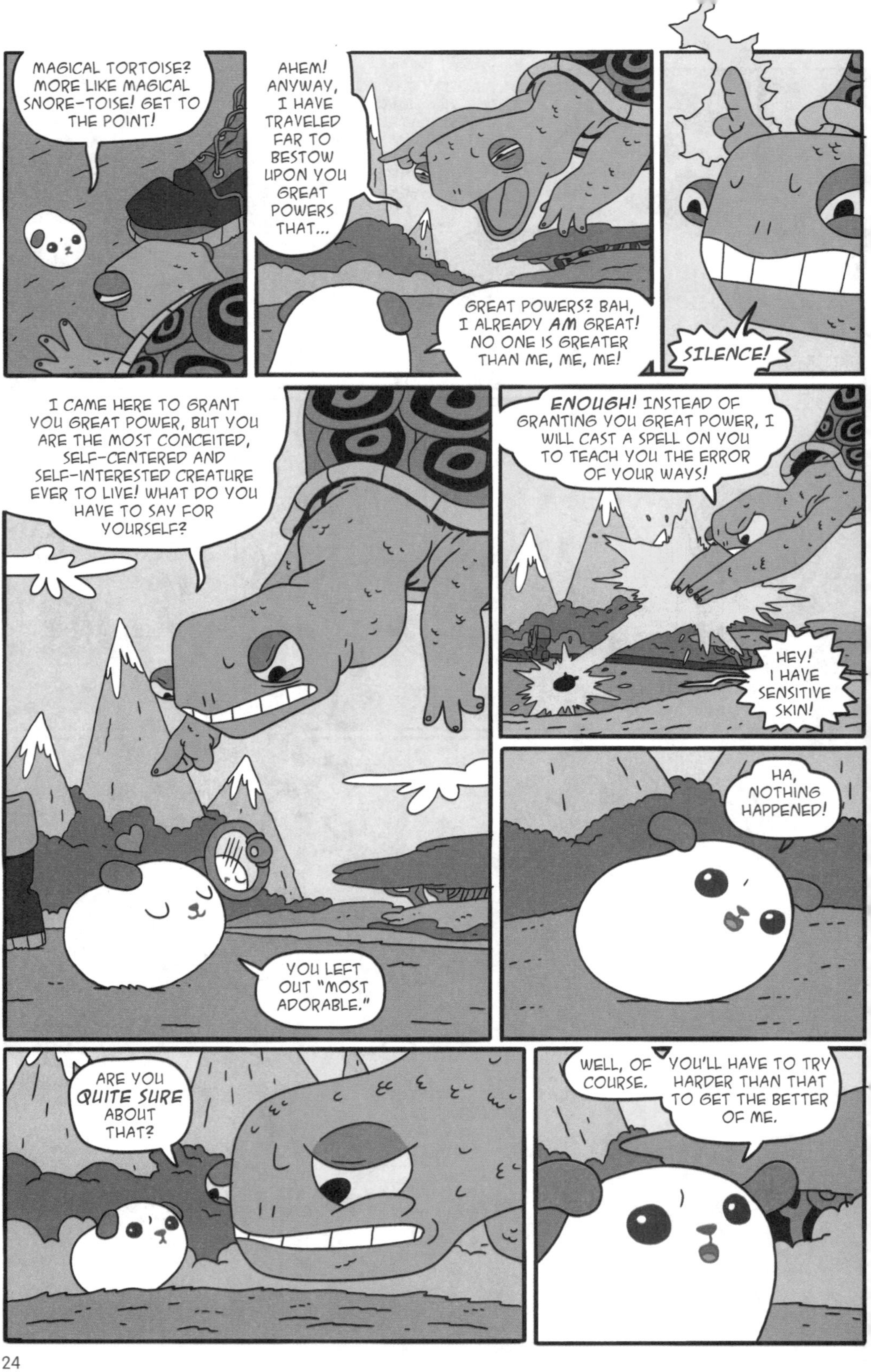
MAGICAL TORTOISE? MORE LIKE MAGICAL SNORE-TOISE! GET TO THE POINT!
AHEM! ANYWAY, I HAVE TRAVELED FAR TO BESTOW UPON YOU GREAT POWERS THAT...
GREAT POWERS? BAH, I ALREADY AM GREAT! NO ONE IS GREATER THAN ME, ME, ME!
SILENCE!
I CAME HERE TO GRANT YOU GREAT POWER, BUT YOU ARE THE MOST CONCEITED, SELF-CENTERED AND SELF-INTERESTED CREATURE EVER TO LIVE! WHAT DO YOU HAVE TO SAY FOR YOURSELF?
YOU LEFT OUT "MOST ADORABLE."
ENOUGH! INSTEAD OF GRANTING YOU GREAT POWER, I WILL CAST A SPELL ON YOU TO TEACH YOU THE ERROR OF YOUR WAYS!
HEY! I HAVE SENSITIVE SKIN!
HA, NOTHING HAPPENED!
ARE YOU QUITE SURE ABOUT THAT?
WELL, OF COURSE.
YOU'LL HAVE TO TRY HARDER THAN THAT TO GET THE BETTER OF ME.

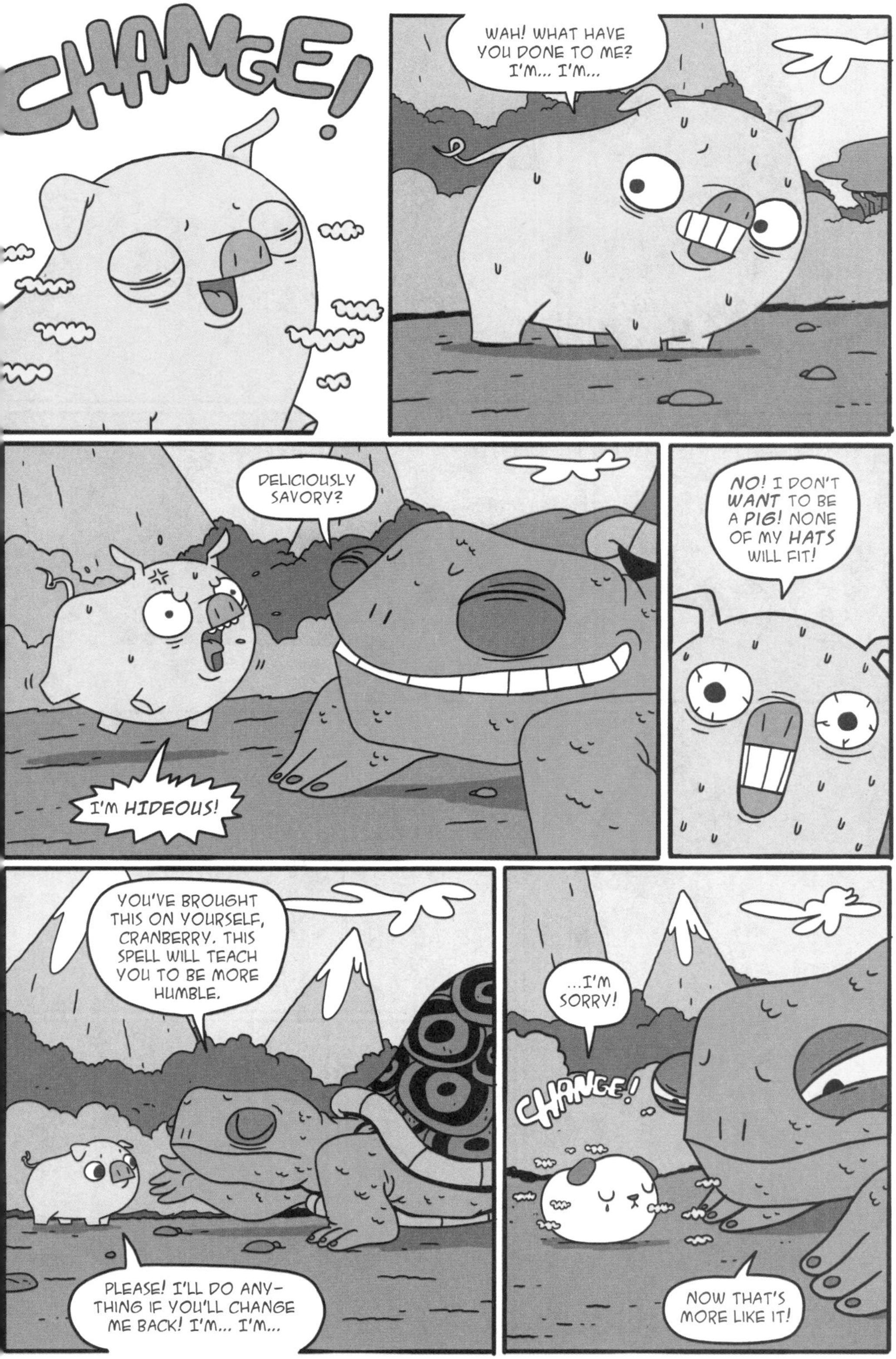
CHANGE!
WAH! WHAT HAVE YOU DONE TO ME? I'M... I'M...
DELICIOUSLY SAVORY?
I'M HIDEOUS!
NO! I DON'T WANT TO BE A PIG! NONE OF MY HATS WILL FIT!
YOU'VE BROUGHT THIS ON YOURSELF, CRANBERRY. THIS SPELL WILL TEACH YOU TO BE MORE HUMBLE.
PLEASE! I'LL DO ANYTHING IF YOU'LL CHANGE ME BACK! I'M... I'M...
...I'M SORRY!
CHANGE!
NOW THAT'S MORE LIKE IT!

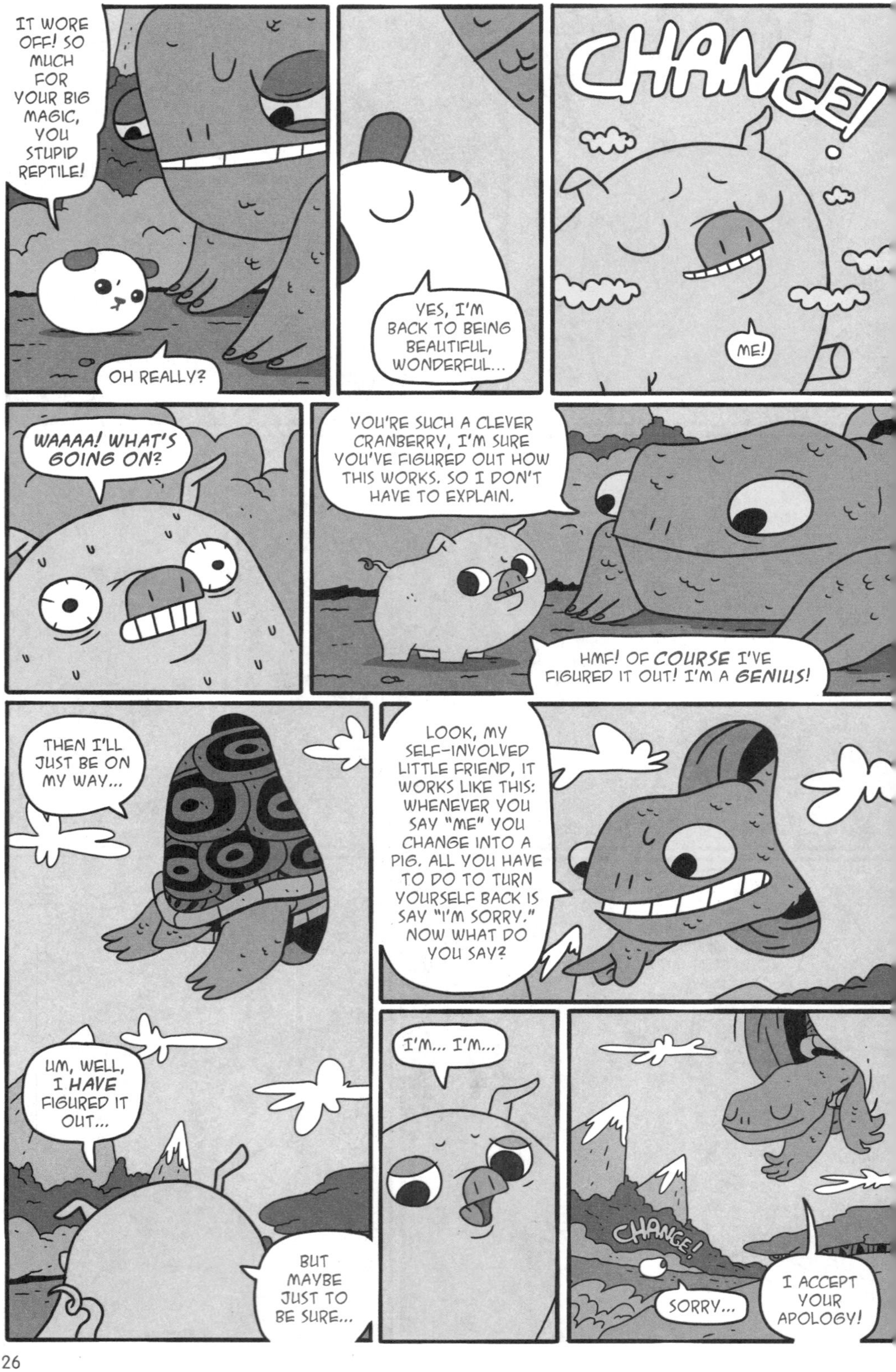
IT WORE OFF! SO MUCH FOR YOUR BIG MAGIC, YOU STUPID REPTILE!
OH REALLY?
YES, I'M BACK TO BEING BEAUTIFUL, WONDERFUL...
CHANGE!
ME!
WAAAA! WHAT'S GOING ON?
YOU'RE SUCH A CLEVER CRANBERRY, I'M SURE YOU'VE FIGURED OUT HOW THIS WORKS. SO I DON'T HAVE TO EXPLAIN.
HMF! OF COURSE I'VE FIGURED IT OUT! I'M A GENIUS!
THEN I'LL JUST BE ON MY WAY...
LOOK, MY SELF-INVOLVED LITTLE FRIEND, IT WORKS LIKE THIS: WHENEVER YOU SAY "ME" YOU CHANGE INTO A PIG. ALL YOU HAVE TO DO TO TURN YOURSELF BACK IS SAY "I'M SORRY." NOW WHAT DO YOU SAY?
UM, WELL, I HAVE FIGURED IT OUT...
BUT MAYBE JUST TO BE SURE...
I'M... I'M...
CHANGE!
SORRY...
I ACCEPT YOUR APOLOGY!

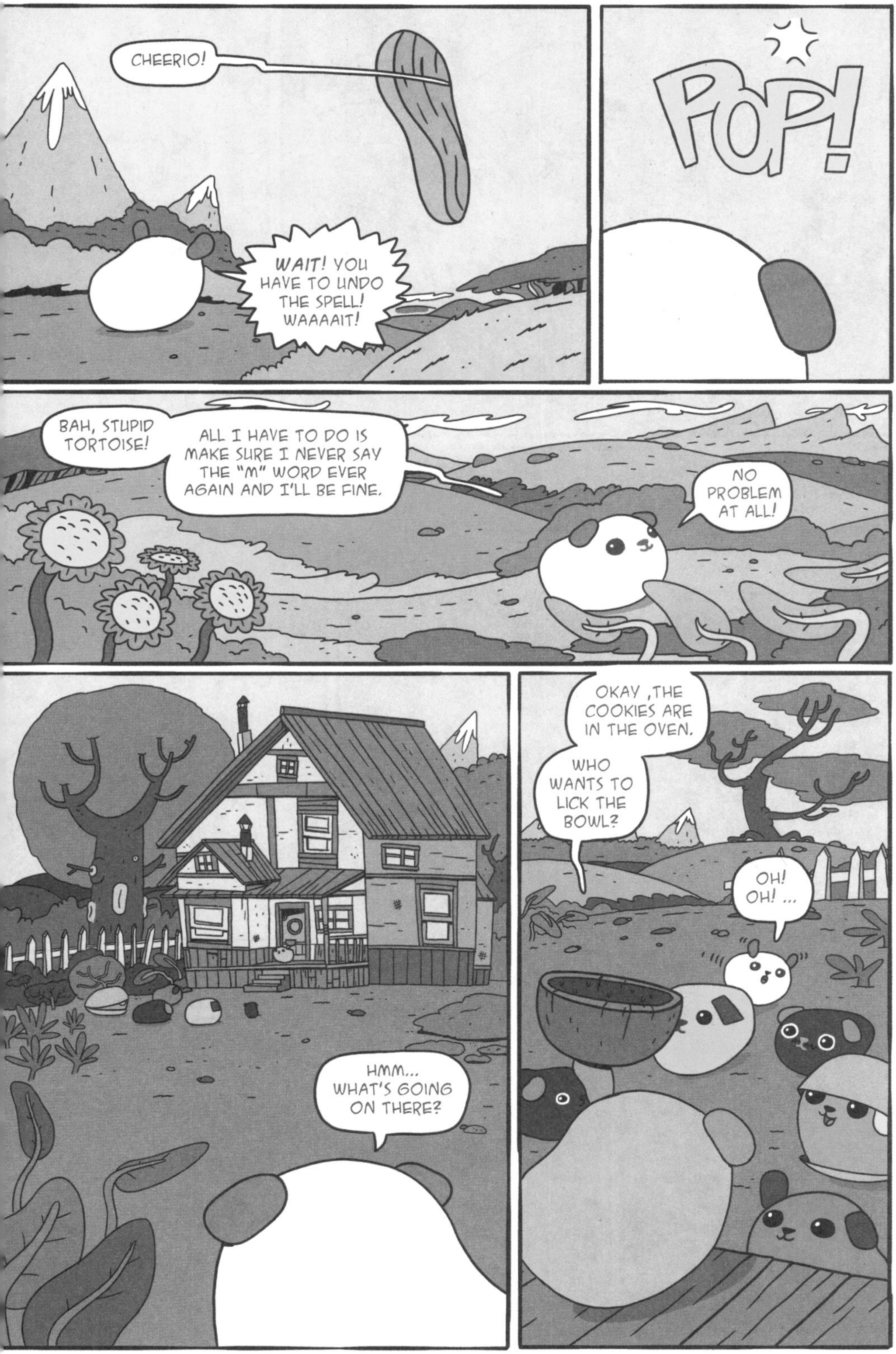
CHEERIO!
WAIT! YOU HAVE TO UNDO THE SPELL! WAAAAIT!
POP!
BAH, STUPID TORTOISE!
ALL I HAVE TO DO IS MAKE SURE I NEVER SAY THE "M" WORD EVER AGAIN AND I'LL BE FINE.
NO PROBLEM AT ALL!
HMM... WHAT'S GOING ON THERE?
OKAY ,THE COOKIES ARE IN THE OVEN.
WHO WANTS TO LICK THE BOWL?
OH! OH! ...

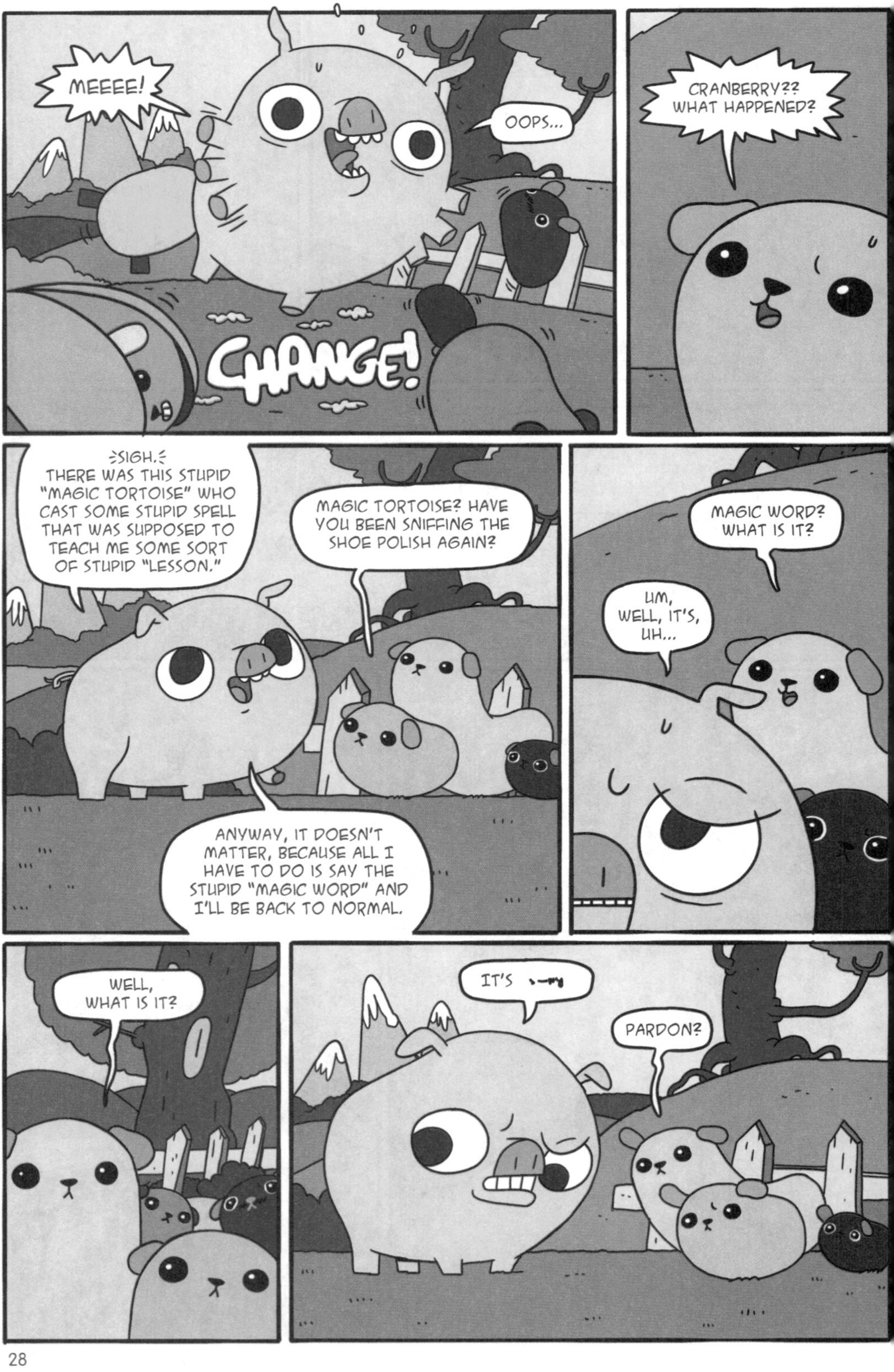
MEEEE!
OOPS...
CHANGE!
CRANBERRY?? WHAT HAPPENED?
SIGH. THERE WAS THIS STUPID "MAGIC TORTOISE" WHO CAST SOME STUPID SPELL THAT WAS SUPPOSED TO TEACH ME SOME SORT OF STUPID "LESSON."
MAGIC TORTOISE? HAVE YOU BEEN SNIFFING THE SHOE POLISH AGAIN?
ANYWAY, IT DOESN'T MATTER, BECAUSE ALL I HAVE TO DO IS SAY THE STUPID "MAGIC WORD" AND I'LL BE BACK TO NORMAL.
MAGIC WORD? WHAT IS IT?
UM, WELL, IT'S, UH...
WELL, WHAT IS IT?
IT'S
PARDON?

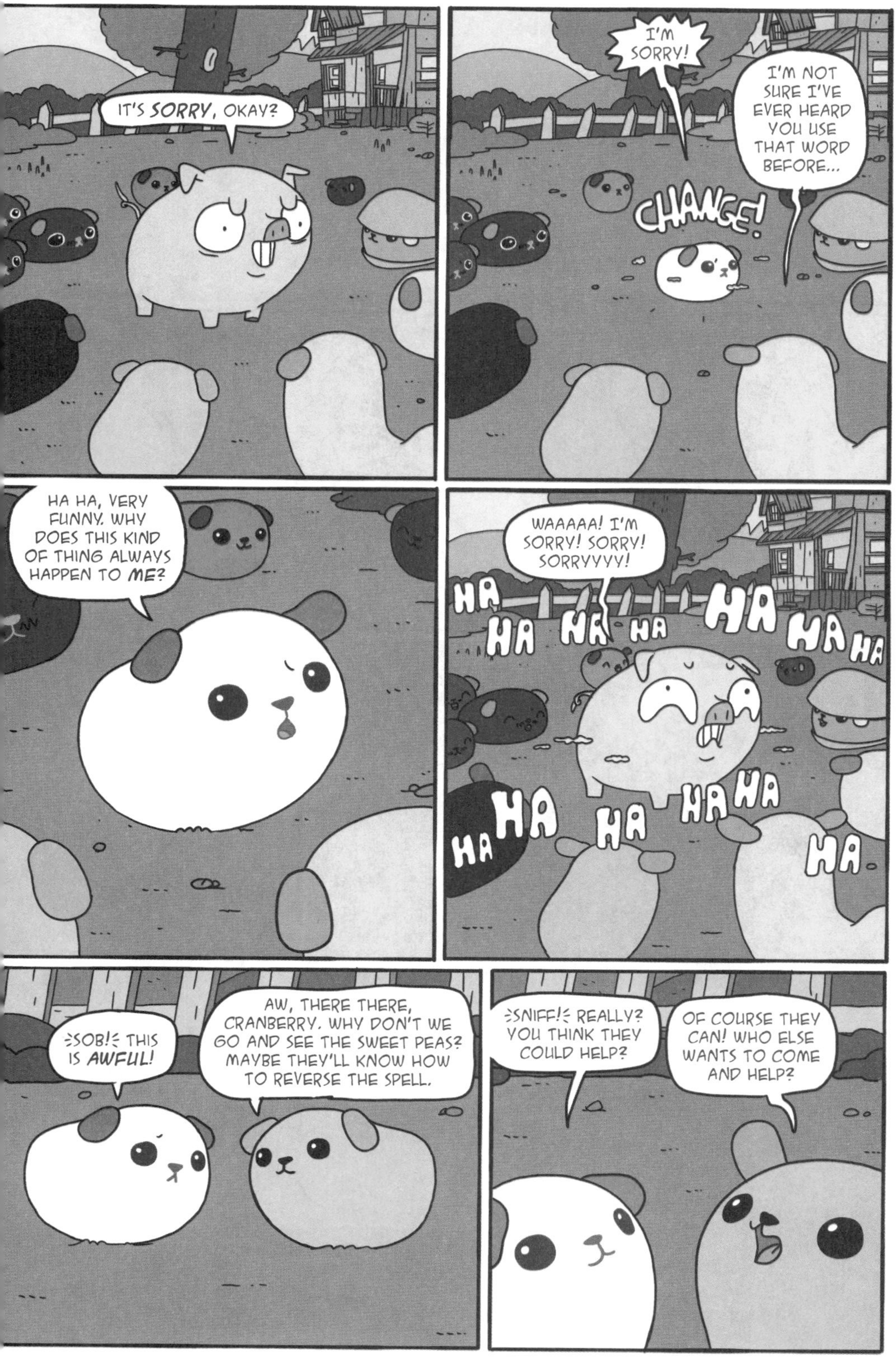
IT'S SORRY, OKAY?
I'M SORRY!
I'M NOT SURE I'VE EVER HEARD YOU USE THAT WORD BEFORE...
CHANGE!
HA HA, VERY FUNNY. WHY DOES THIS KIND OF THING ALWAYS HAPPEN TO ME?
WAAAAAA! I'M SORRY! SORRY! SORRYYYY!
HA HA HA HA HA HA HA HA HA HA HA HA HA HA
≈SOB!≈ THIS IS AWFUL!
AW, THERE THERE, CRANBERRY. WHY DON'T WE GO AND SEE THE SWEET PEAS? MAYBE THEY'LL KNOW HOW TO REVERSE THE SPELL.
≈SNIFF!≈ REALLY? YOU THINK THEY COULD HELP?
OF COURSE THEY CAN! WHO ELSE WANTS TO COME AND HELP?

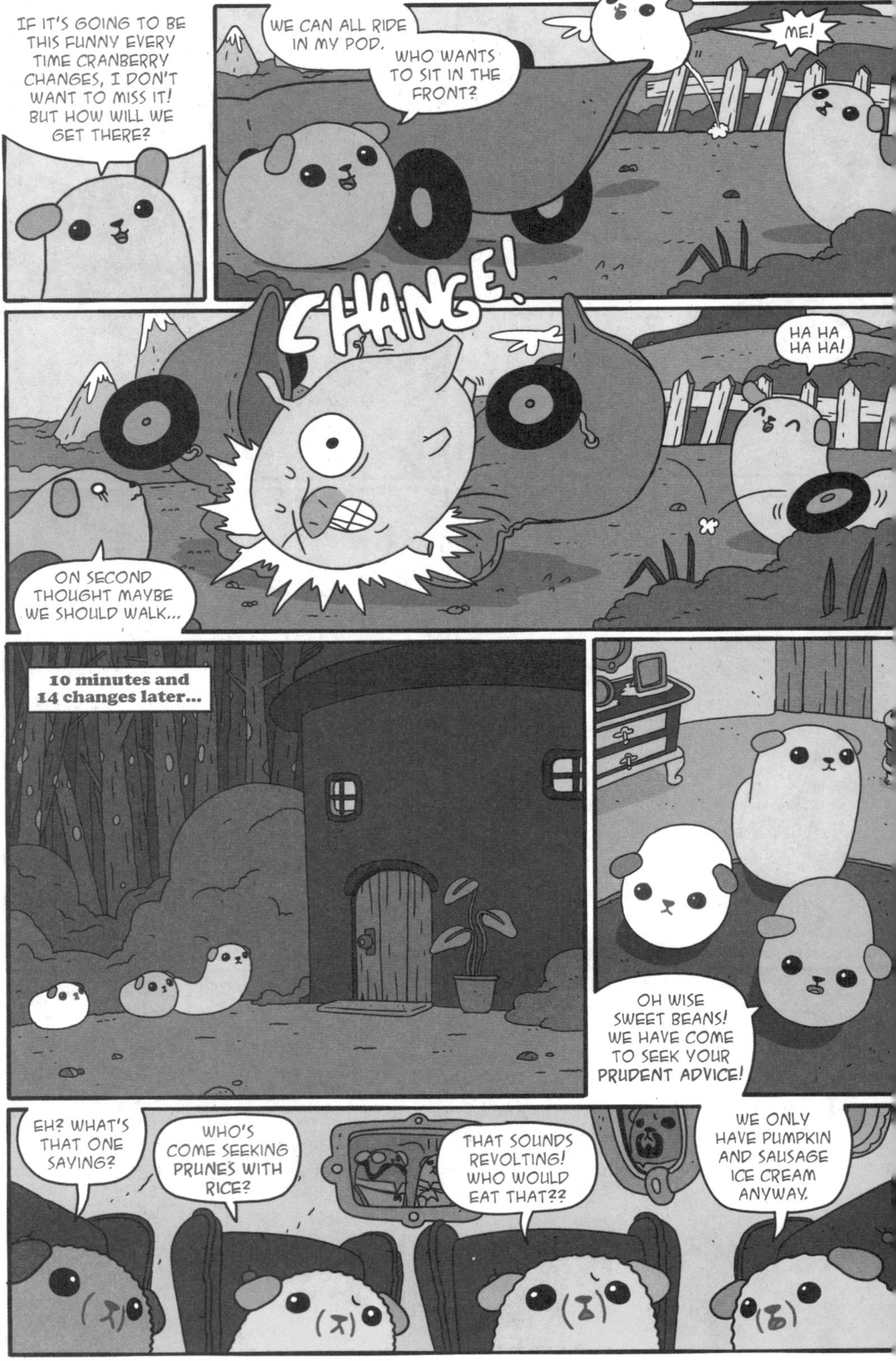
IF IT'S GOING TO BE THIS FUNNY EVERY TIME CRANBERRY CHANGES, I DON'T WANT TO MISS IT! BUT HOW WILL WE GET THERE?
WE CAN ALL RIDE IN MY POD.
WHO WANTS TO SIT IN THE FRONT?
ME!
CHANGE!
HA HA HA HA!
ON SECOND THOUGHT MAYBE WE SHOULD WALK...
10 minutes and 14 changes later...
OH WISE SWEET BEANS! WE HAVE COME TO SEEK YOUR PRUDENT ADVICE!
EH? WHAT'S THAT ONE SAYING?
WHO'S COME SEEKING PRUNES WITH RICE?
THAT SOUNDS REVOLTING! WHO WOULD EAT THAT??
WE ONLY HAVE PUMPKIN AND SAUSAGE ICE CREAM ANYWAY.

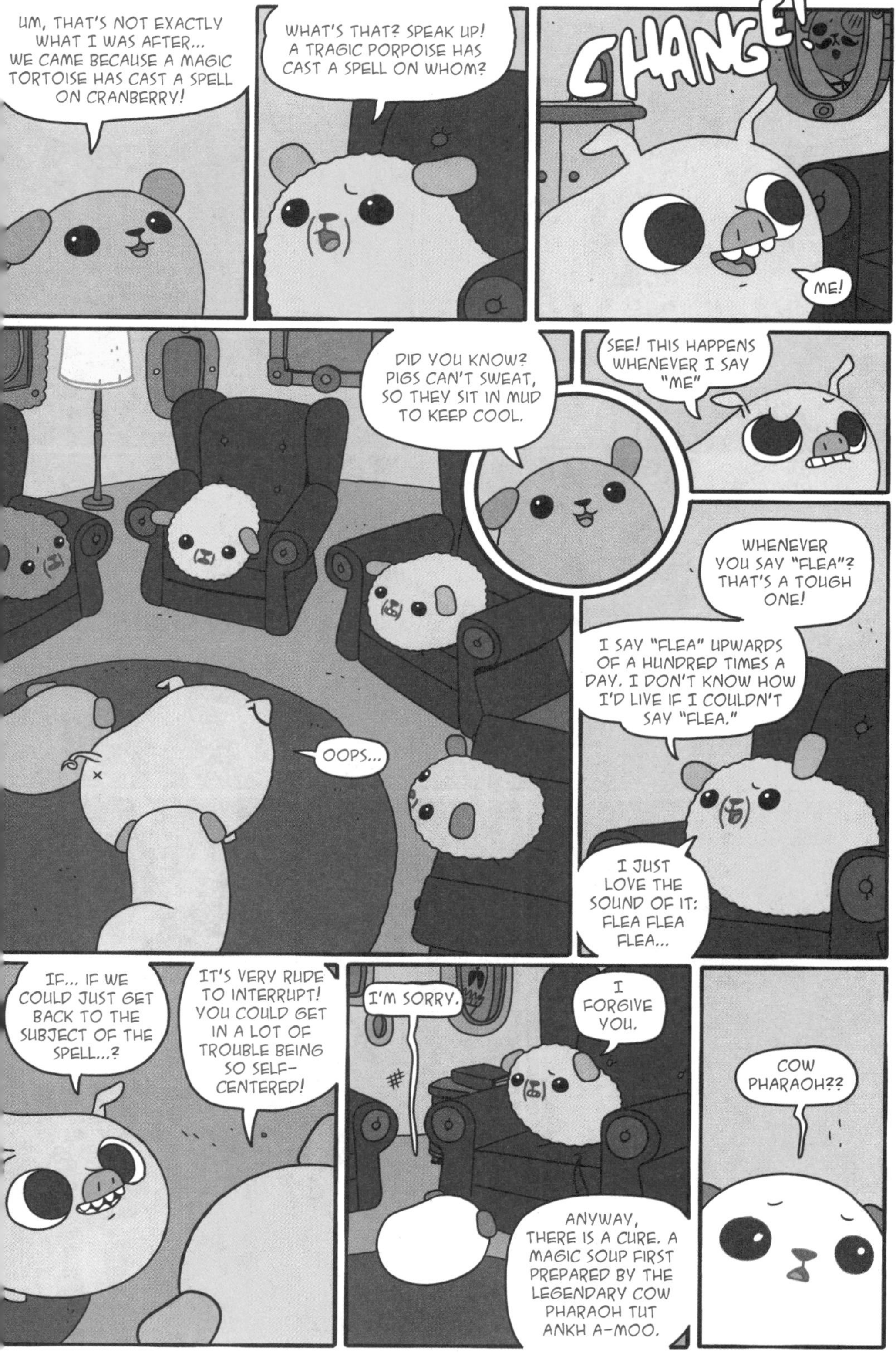
UM, THAT'S NOT EXACTLY WHAT I WAS AFTER... WE CAME BECAUSE A MAGIC TORTOISE HAS CAST A SPELL ON CRANBERRY!
WHAT'S THAT? SPEAK UP! A TRAGIC PORPOISE HAS CAST A SPELL ON WHOM?
CHANGE!
ME!
DID YOU KNOW? PIGS CAN'T SWEAT, SO THEY SIT IN MUD TO KEEP COOL.
SEE! THIS HAPPENS WHENEVER I SAY "ME"
OOPS...
WHENEVER YOU SAY "FLEA"? THAT'S A TOUGH ONE!
I SAY "FLEA" UPWARDS OF A HUNDRED TIMES A DAY. I DON'T KNOW HOW I'D LIVE IF I COULDN'T SAY "FLEA."
I JUST LOVE THE SOUND OF IT: FLEA FLEA FLEA...
IF... IF WE COULD JUST GET BACK TO THE SUBJECT OF THE SPELL...?
IT'S VERY RUDE TO INTERRUPT! YOU COULD GET IN A LOT OF TROUBLE BEING SO SELF-CENTERED!
I'M SORRY.
I FORGIVE YOU.
ANYWAY, THERE IS A CURE. A MAGIC SOUP FIRST PREPARED BY THE LEGENDARY COW PHARAOH TUT ANKH A-MOO.
COW PHARAOH??

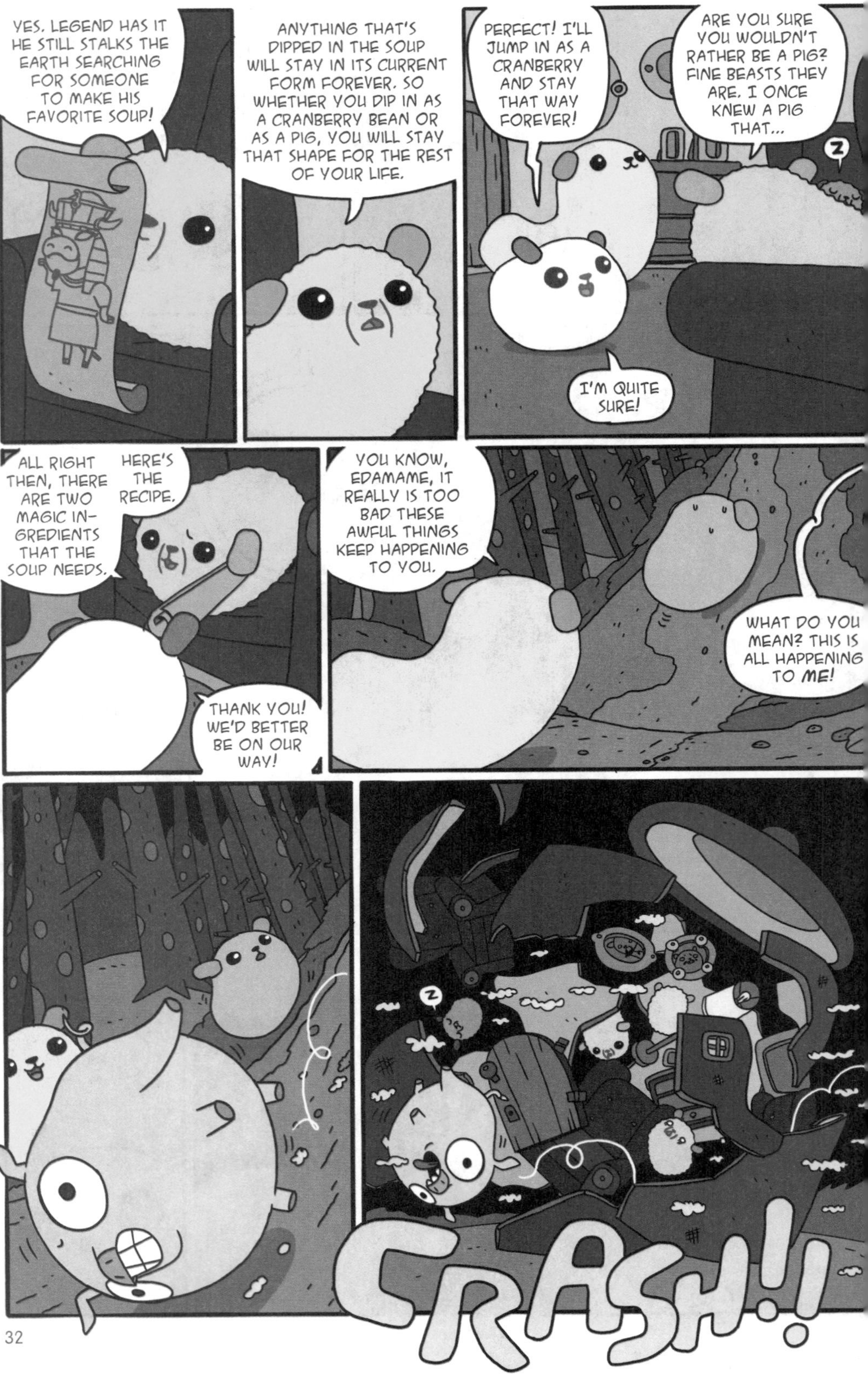
YES. LEGEND HAS IT HE STILL STALKS THE EARTH SEARCHING FOR SOMEONE TO MAKE HIS FAVORITE SOUP!
ANYTHING THAT'S DIPPED IN THE SOUP WILL STAY IN ITS CURRENT FORM FOREVER. SO WHETHER YOU DIP IN AS A CRANBERRY BEAN OR AS A PIG, YOU WILL STAY THAT SHAPE FOR THE REST OF YOUR LIFE.
PERFECT! I'LL JUMP IN AS A CRANBERRY AND STAY THAT WAY FOREVER!
ARE YOU SURE YOU WOULDN'T RATHER BE A PIG? FINE BEASTS THEY ARE. I ONCE KNEW A PIG THAT...
Z
I'M QUITE SURE!
ALL RIGHT THEN, THERE ARE TWO MAGIC IN-GREDIENTS THAT THE SOUP NEEDS.
HERE'S THE RECIPE.
THANK YOU! WE'D BETTER BE ON OUR WAY!
YOU KNOW, EDAMAME, IT REALLY IS TOO BAD THESE AWFUL THINGS KEEP HAPPENING TO YOU.
WHAT DO YOU MEAN? THIS IS ALL HAPPENING TO **ME**!
Z
CRASH!!

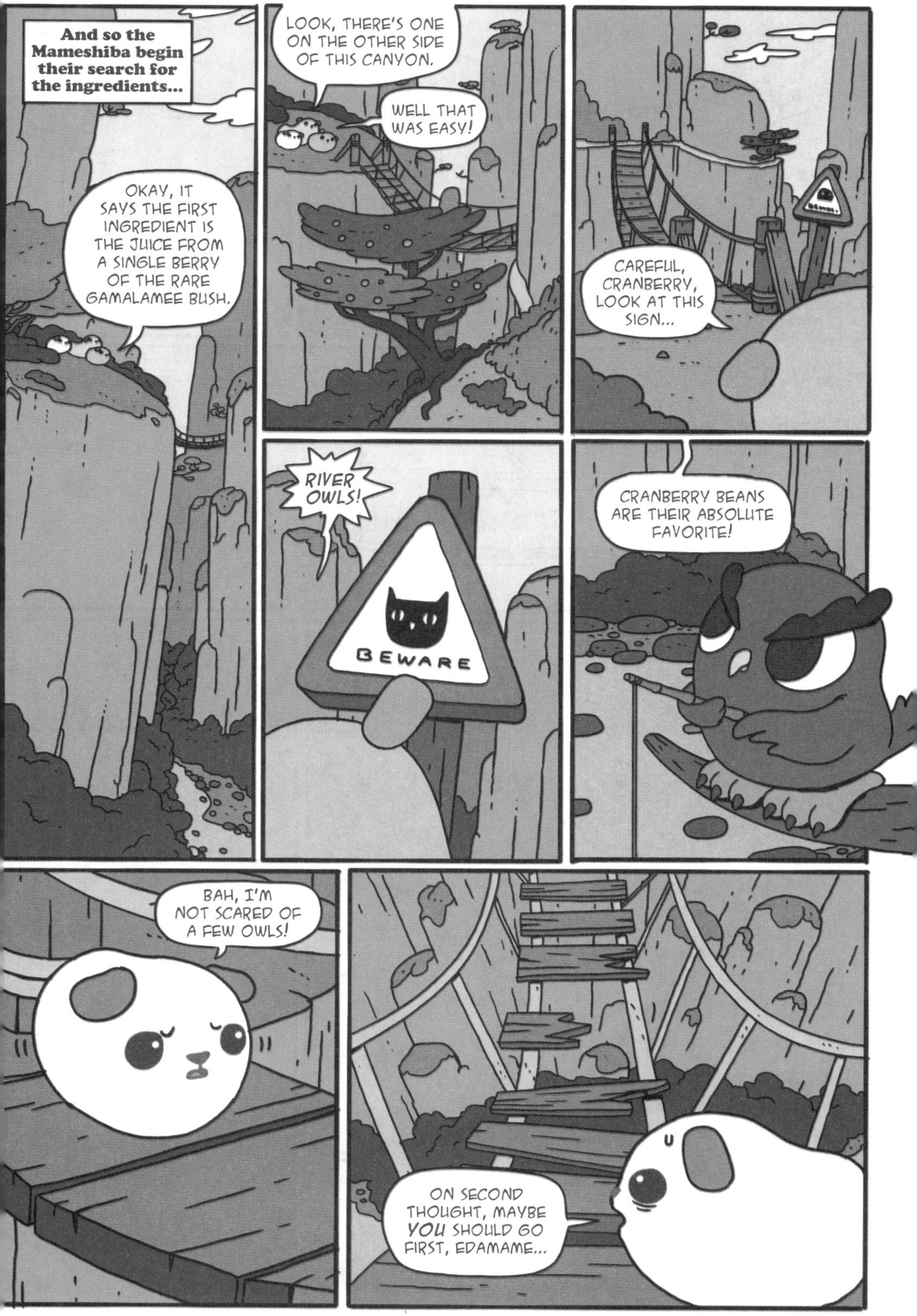
And so the Mameshiba begin their search for the ingredients...
OKAY, IT SAYS THE FIRST INGREDIENT IS THE JUICE FROM A SINGLE BERRY OF THE RARE GAMALAMEE BUSH.
LOOK, THERE'S ONE ON THE OTHER SIDE OF THIS CANYON.
WELL THAT WAS EASY!
CAREFUL, CRANBERRY, LOOK AT THIS SIGN...
RIVER OWLS!
BEWARE
CRANBERRY BEANS ARE THEIR ABSOLUTE FAVORITE!
BAH, I'M NOT SCARED OF A FEW OWLS!
ON SECOND THOUGHT, MAYBE YOU SHOULD GO FIRST, EDAMAME...

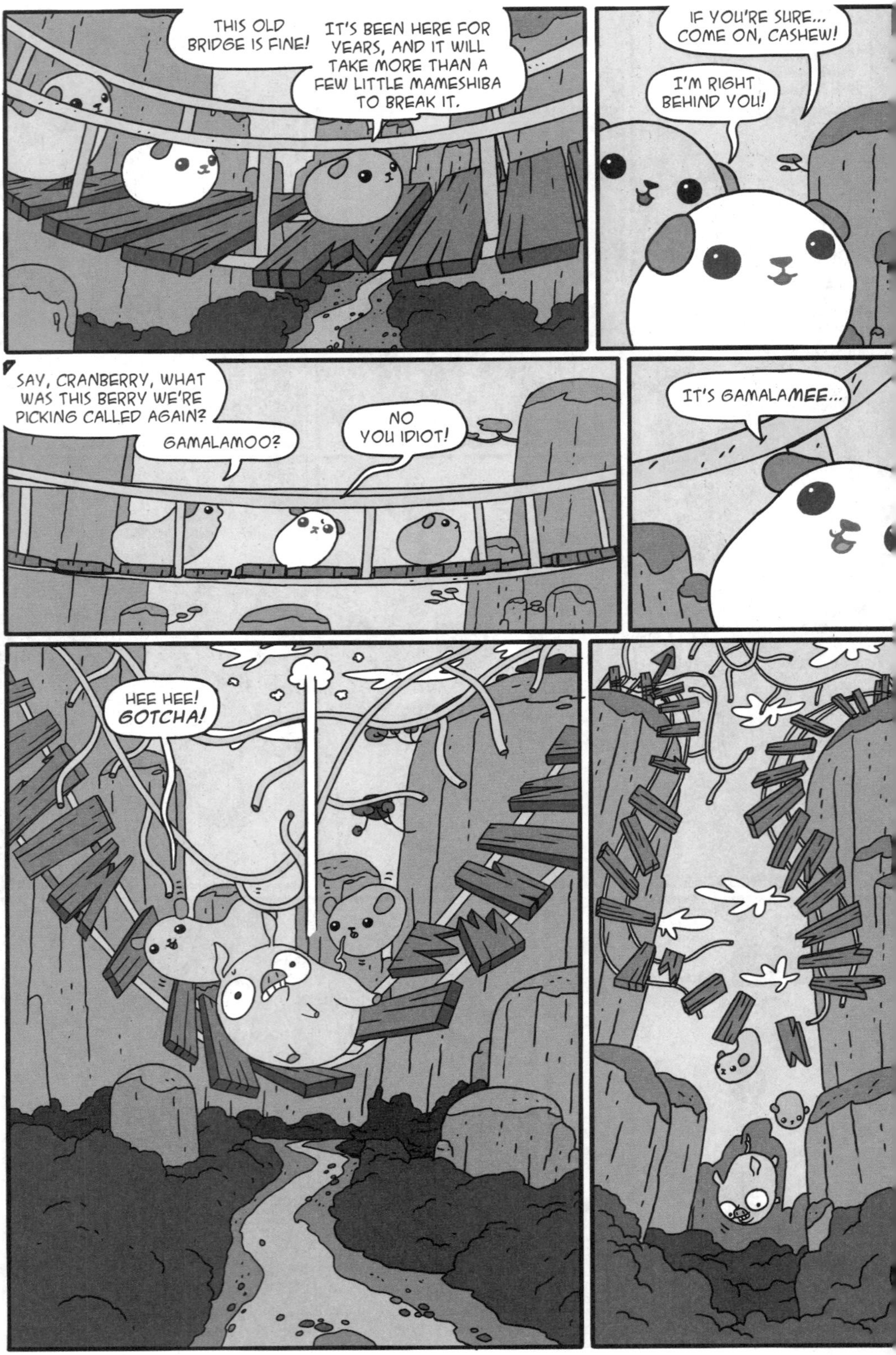
THIS OLD BRIDGE IS FINE!
IT'S BEEN HERE FOR YEARS, AND IT WILL TAKE MORE THAN A FEW LITTLE MAMESHIBA TO BREAK IT.
IF YOU'RE SURE... COME ON, CASHEW!
I'M RIGHT BEHIND YOU!
SAY, CRANBERRY, WHAT WAS THIS BERRY WE'RE PICKING CALLED AGAIN?
GAMALAMOO?
NO YOU IDIOT!
IT'S GAMALAMEE...
HEE HEE! GOTCHA!

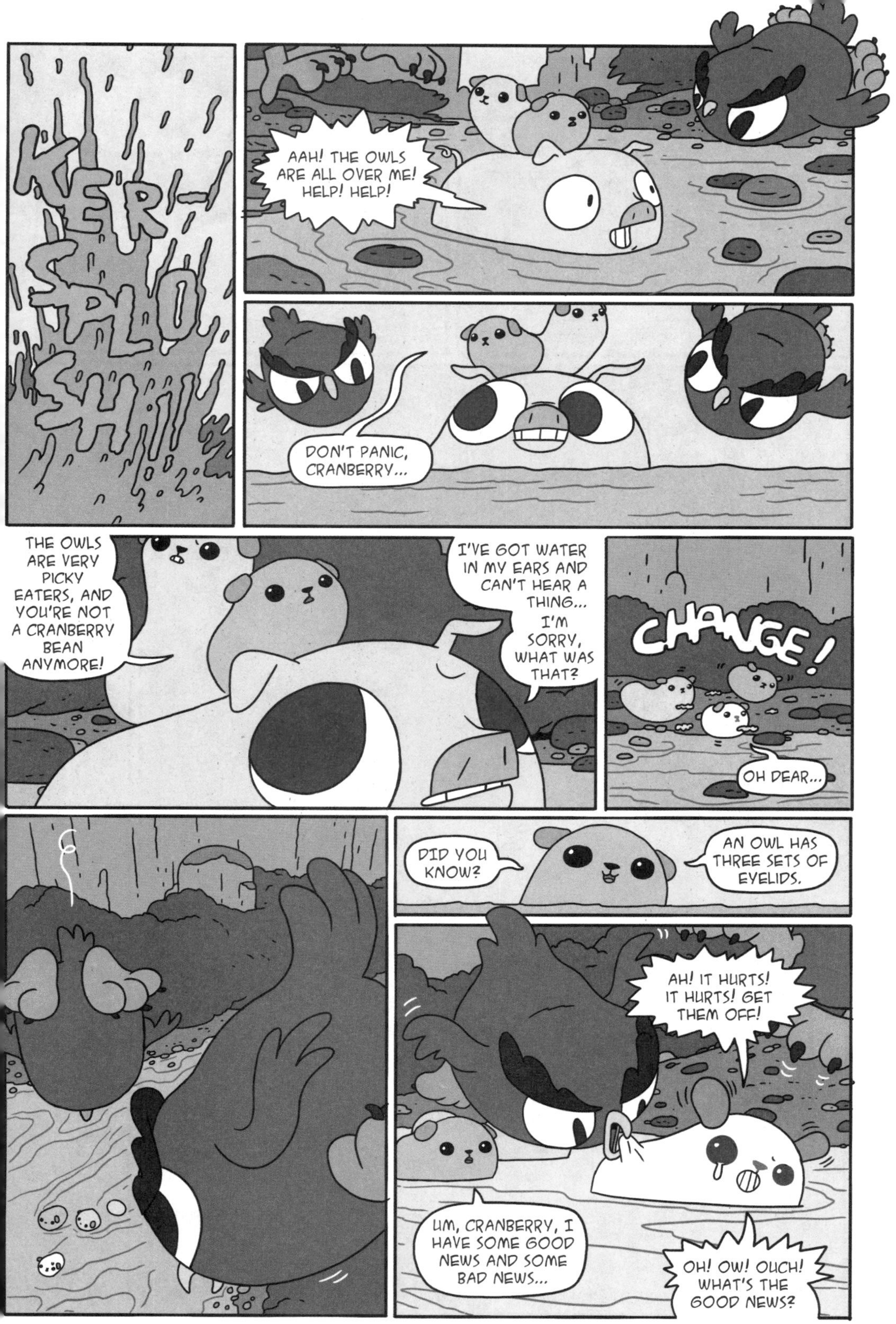
KER-SPLOSH!
AAH! THE OWLS ARE ALL OVER ME! HELP! HELP!
DON'T PANIC, CRANBERRY...
THE OWLS ARE VERY PICKY EATERS, AND YOU'RE NOT A CRANBERRY BEAN ANYMORE!
I'VE GOT WATER IN MY EARS AND CAN'T HEAR A THING...
I'M SORRY, WHAT WAS THAT?
CHANGE!
OH DEAR...
DID YOU KNOW?
AN OWL HAS THREE SETS OF EYELIDS.
AH! IT HURTS! IT HURTS! GET THEM OFF!
UM, CRANBERRY, I HAVE SOME GOOD NEWS AND SOME BAD NEWS...
OH! OW! OUCH! WHAT'S THE GOOD NEWS?

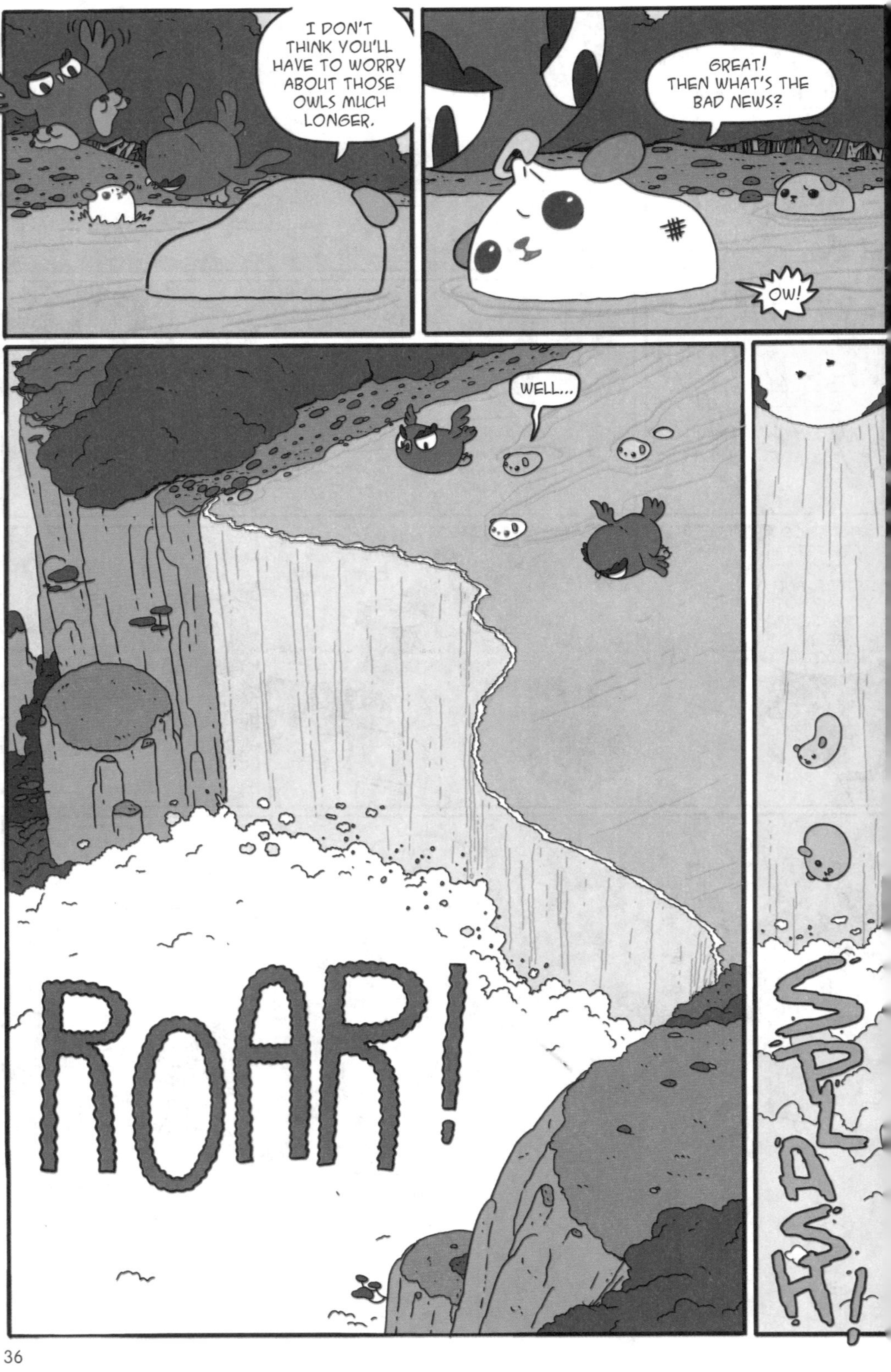
I DON'T THINK YOU'LL HAVE TO WORRY ABOUT THOSE OWLS MUCH LONGER.
GREAT! THEN WHAT'S THE BAD NEWS?
OW!
WELL...
ROAR!
SPLASH!

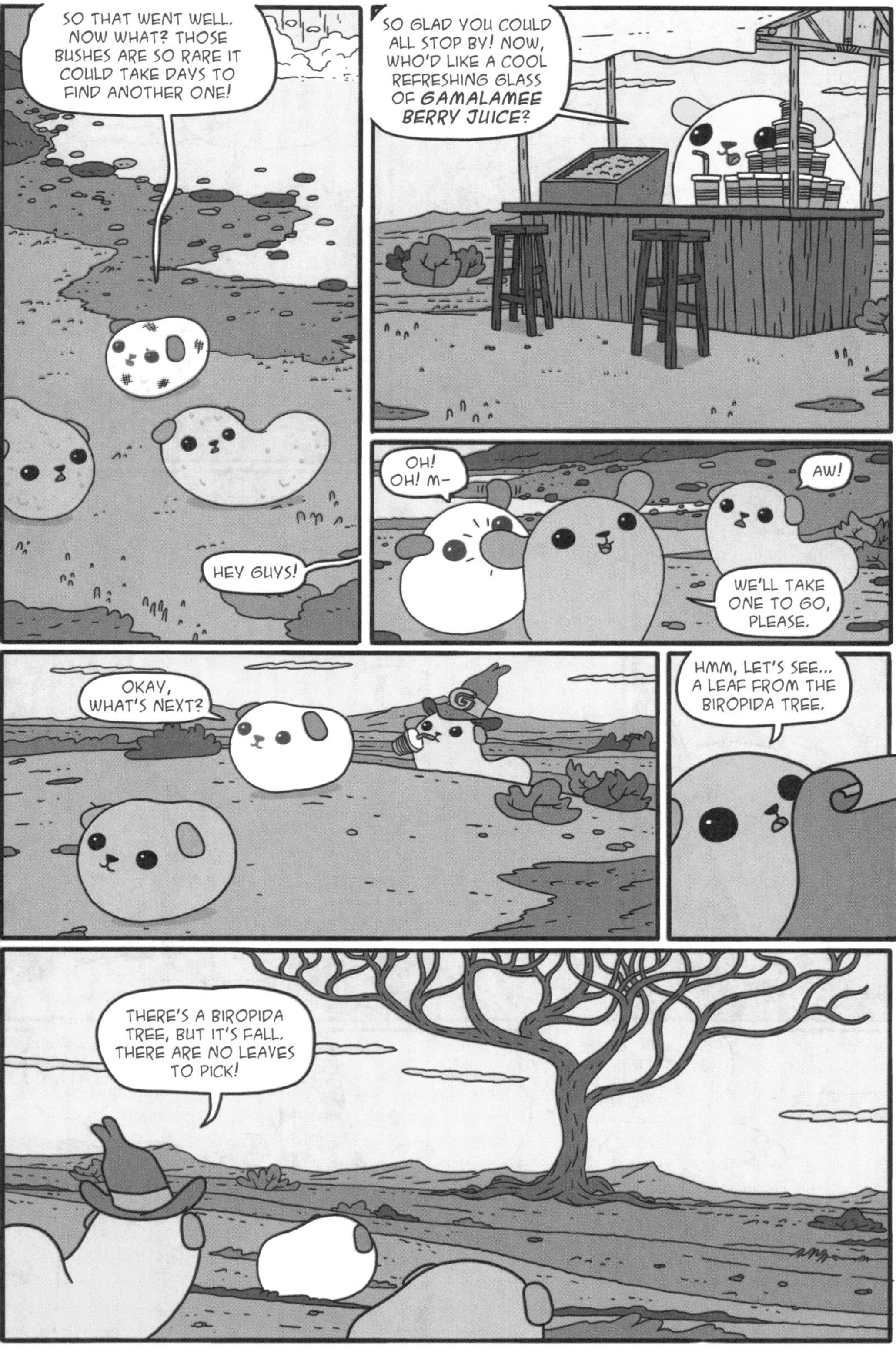
SO THAT WENT WELL. NOW WHAT? THOSE BUSHES ARE SO RARE IT COULD TAKE DAYS TO FIND ANOTHER ONE!
HEY GUYS!
SO GLAD YOU COULD ALL STOP BY! NOW, WHO'D LIKE A COOL REFRESHING GLASS OF **GAMALAMEE BERRY JUICE**?
OH! OH! M-
AW!
WE'LL TAKE ONE TO GO, PLEASE.
OKAY, WHAT'S NEXT?
HMM, LET'S SEE... A LEAF FROM THE BIROPIDA TREE.
THERE'S A BIROPIDA TREE, BUT IT'S FALL. THERE ARE NO LEAVES TO PICK!

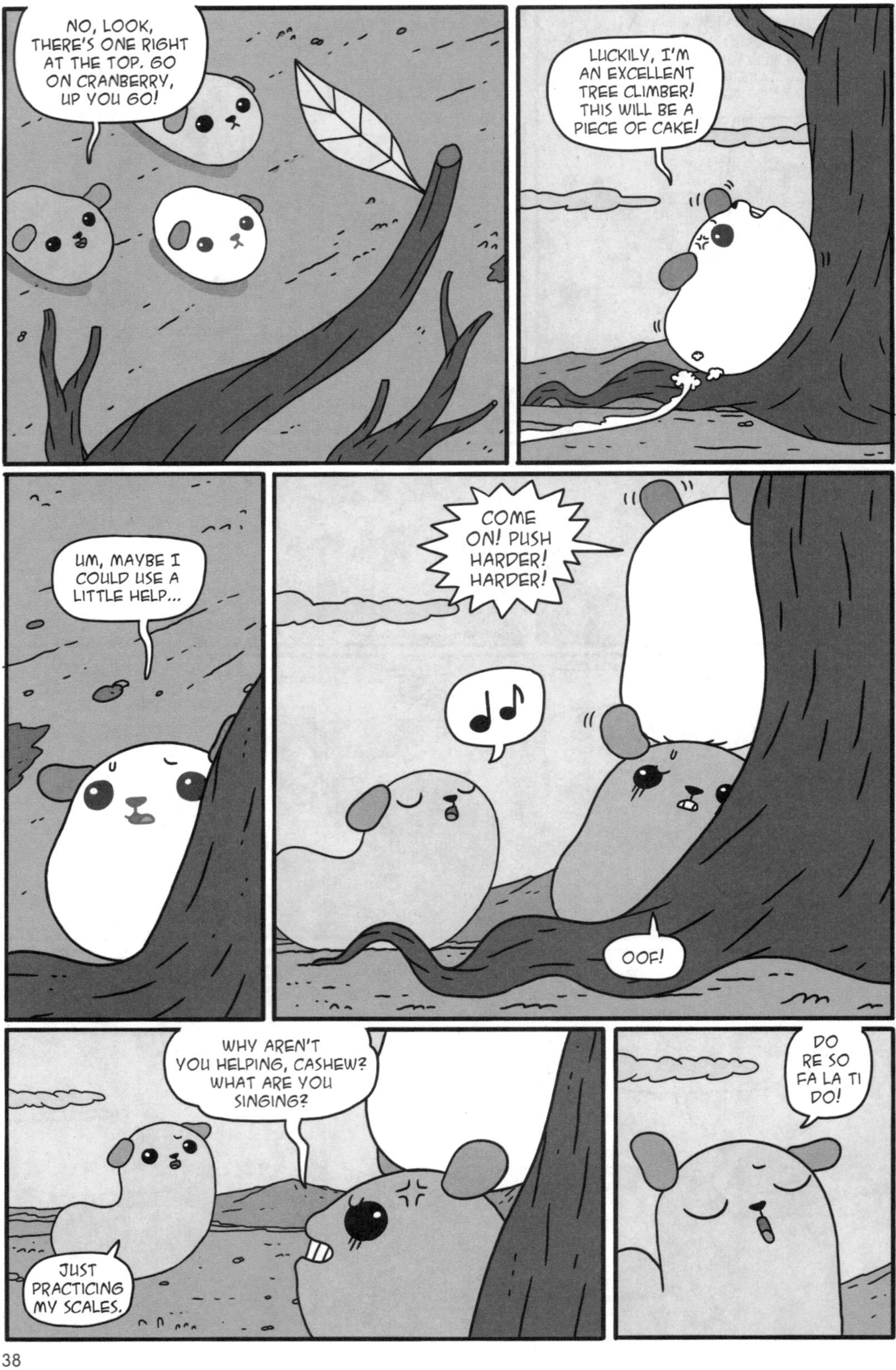
NO, LOOK, THERE'S ONE RIGHT AT THE TOP. GO ON CRANBERRY, UP YOU GO!
LUCKILY, I'M AN EXCELLENT TREE CLIMBER! THIS WILL BE A PIECE OF CAKE!
UM, MAYBE I COULD USE A LITTLE HELP...
COME ON! PUSH HARDER! HARDER!
OOF!
WHY AREN'T YOU HELPING, CASHEW? WHAT ARE YOU SINGING?
JUST PRACTICING MY SCALES.
DO RE SO FA LA TI DO!

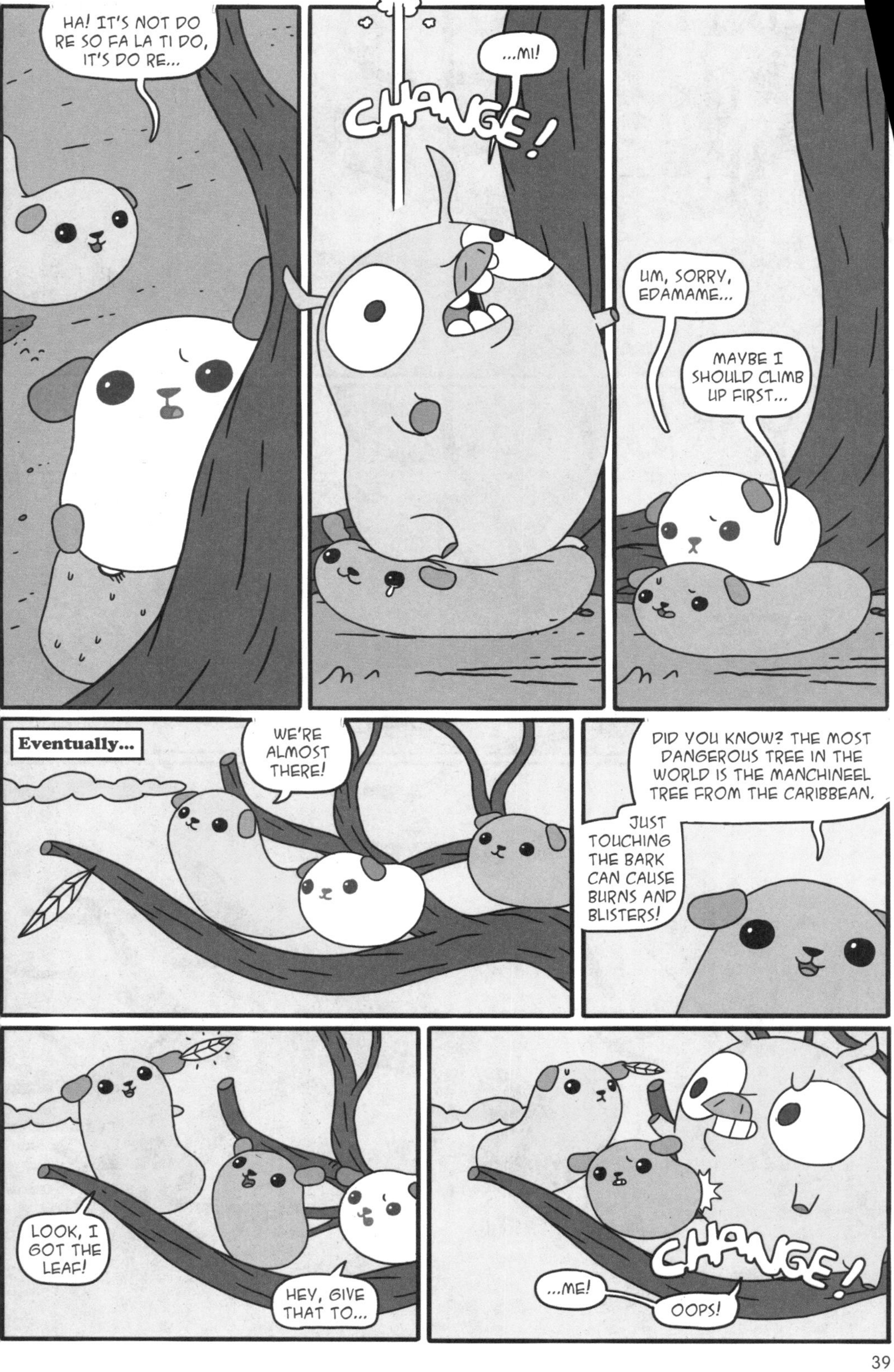
HA! IT'S NOT DO RE SO FA LA TI DO, IT'S DO RE...
...MI!
CHANGE!
UM, SORRY, EDAMAME...
MAYBE I SHOULD CLIMB UP FIRST...
Eventually...
WE'RE ALMOST THERE!
DID YOU KNOW? THE MOST DANGEROUS TREE IN THE WORLD IS THE MANCHINEEL TREE FROM THE CARIBBEAN.
JUST TOUCHING THE BARK CAN CAUSE BURNS AND BLISTERS!
LOOK, I GOT THE LEAF!
HEY, GIVE THAT TO...
CHANGE!
...ME!
OOPS!

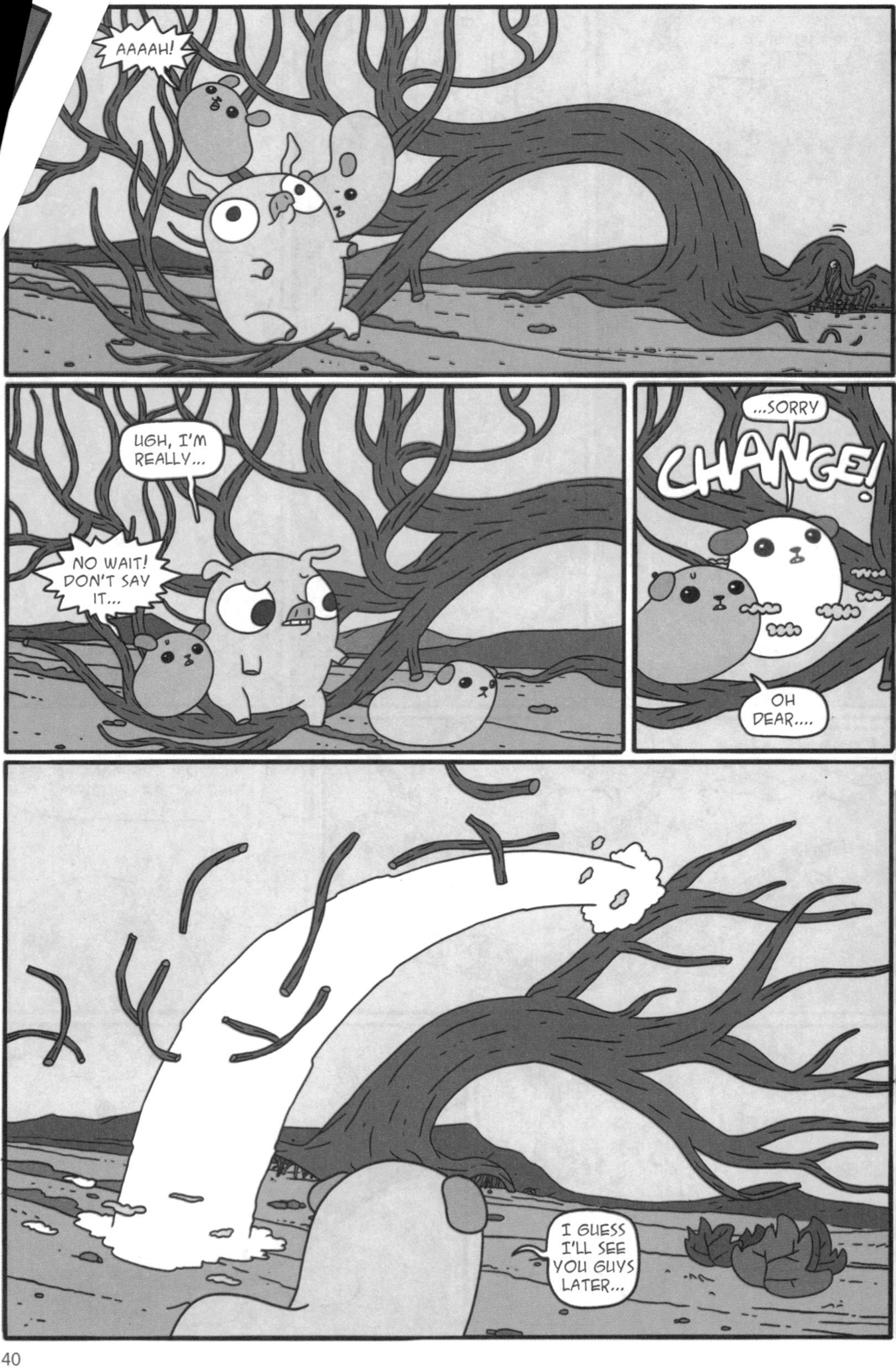
AAAAH!
UGH, I'M REALLY...
NO WAIT! DON'T SAY IT...
...SORRY
CHANGE!
OH DEAR....
I GUESS I'LL SEE YOU GUYS LATER...

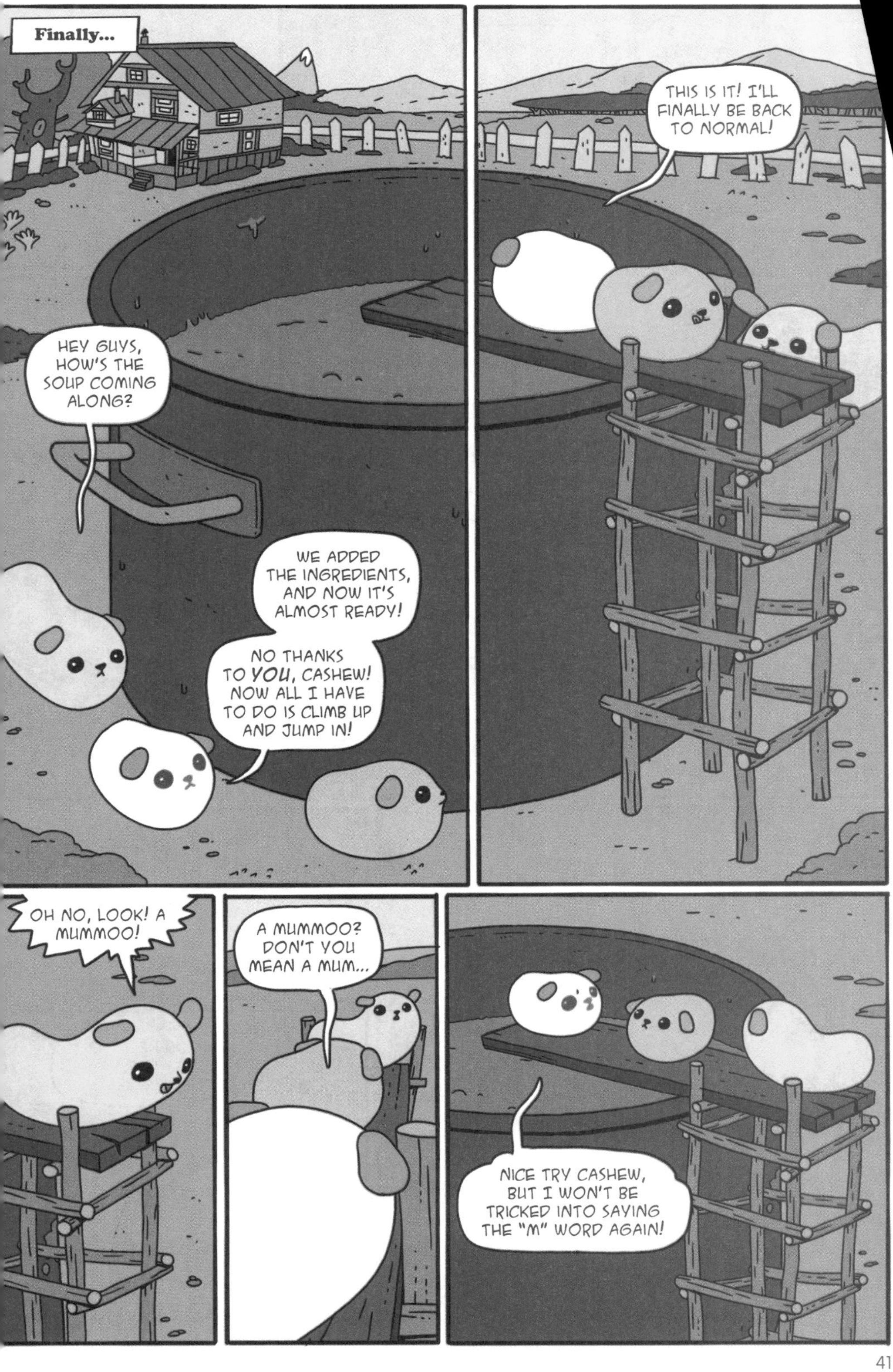
Finally...
HEY GUYS, HOW'S THE SOUP COMING ALONG?
WE ADDED THE INGREDIENTS, AND NOW IT'S ALMOST READY!
NO THANKS TO YOU, CASHEW! NOW ALL I HAVE TO DO IS CLIMB UP AND JUMP IN!
THIS IS IT! I'LL FINALLY BE BACK TO NORMAL!
OH NO, LOOK! A MUMMOO!
A MUMMOO? DON'T YOU MEAN A MUM...
NICE TRY CASHEW, BUT I WON'T BE TRICKED INTO SAYING THE "M" WORD AGAIN!

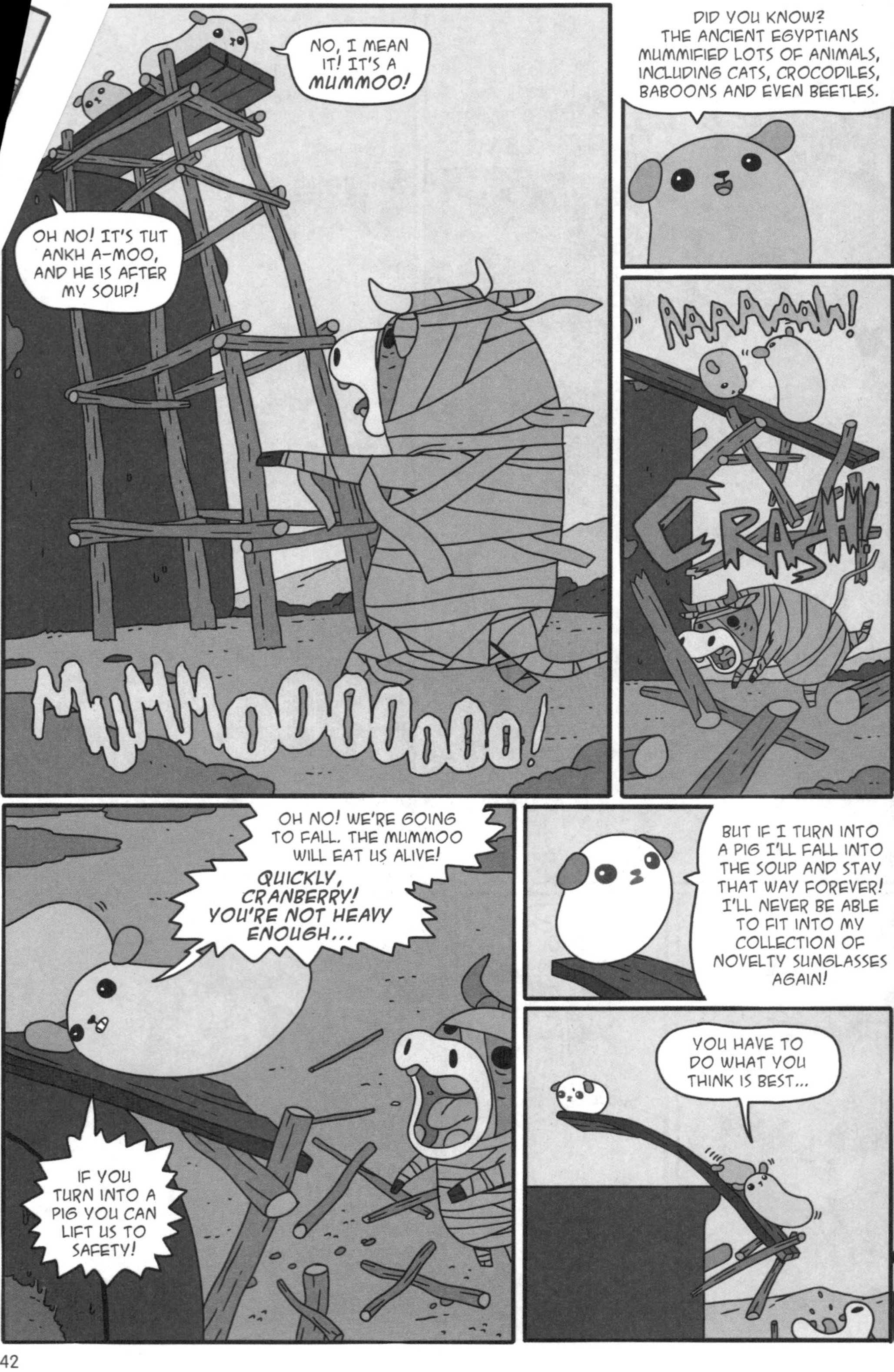
NO, I MEAN IT! IT'S A MUMMOO!
OH NO! IT'S TUT ANKH A-MOO, AND HE IS AFTER MY SOUP!
MUMMOOOOOOOO!
DID YOU KNOW? THE ANCIENT EGYPTIANS MUMMIFIED LOTS OF ANIMALS, INCLUDING CATS, CROCODILES, BABOONS AND EVEN BEETLES.
AAAAAAH!
CRASH!
OH NO! WE'RE GOING TO FALL. THE MUMMOO WILL EAT US ALIVE!
QUICKLY, CRANBERRY! YOU'RE NOT HEAVY ENOUGH...
IF YOU TURN INTO A PIG YOU CAN LIFT US TO SAFETY!
BUT IF I TURN INTO A PIG I'LL FALL INTO THE SOUP AND STAY THAT WAY FOREVER! I'LL NEVER BE ABLE TO FIT INTO MY COLLECTION OF NOVELTY SUNGLASSES AGAIN!
YOU HAVE TO DO WHAT YOU THINK IS BEST...

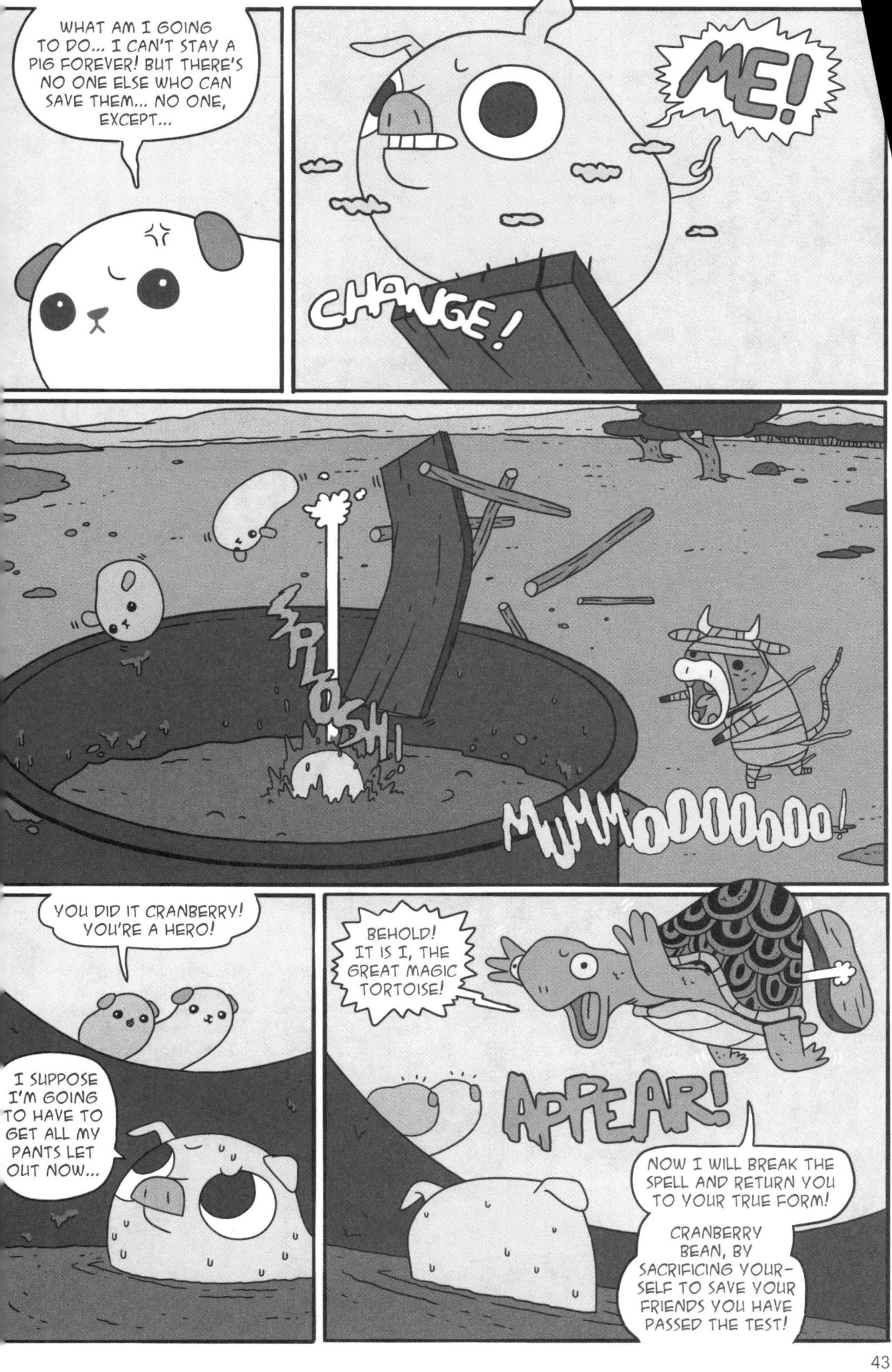
WHAT AM I GOING TO DO... I CAN'T STAY A PIG FOREVER! BUT THERE'S NO ONE ELSE WHO CAN SAVE THEM... NO ONE, EXCEPT...
ME!
CHANGE!
SPLOOSH!
MUMMOOOOOooo!
YOU DID IT CRANBERRY! YOU'RE A HERO!
I SUPPOSE I'M GOING TO HAVE TO GET ALL MY PANTS LET OUT NOW...
BEHOLD! IT IS I, THE GREAT MAGIC TORTOISE!
APPEAR!
NOW I WILL BREAK THE SPELL AND RETURN YOU TO YOUR TRUE FORM!
CRANBERRY BEAN, BY SACRIFICING YOURSELF TO SAVE YOUR FRIENDS YOU HAVE PASSED THE TEST!

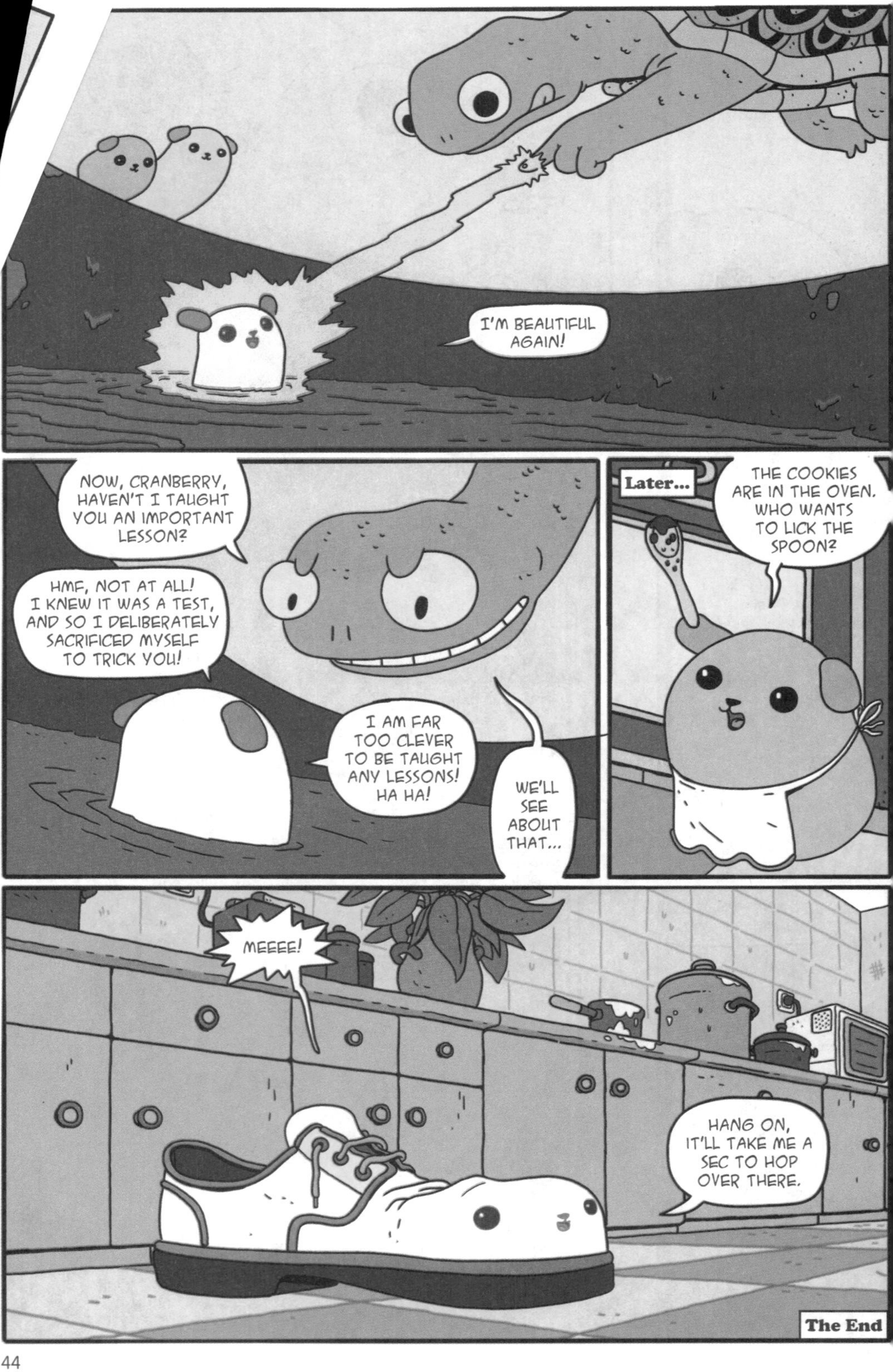
I'M BEAUTIFUL AGAIN!
NOW, CRANBERRY, HAVEN'T I TAUGHT YOU AN IMPORTANT LESSON?
HMF, NOT AT ALL! I KNEW IT WAS A TEST, AND SO I DELIBERATELY SACRIFICED MYSELF TO TRICK YOU!
I AM FAR TOO CLEVER TO BE TAUGHT ANY LESSONS! HA HA!
WE'LL SEE ABOUT THAT...
Later...
THE COOKIES ARE IN THE OVEN. WHO WANTS TO LICK THE SPOON?
MEEEE!
HANG ON, IT'LL TAKE ME A SEC TO HOP OVER THERE.
The End

One Enchanted Evening...

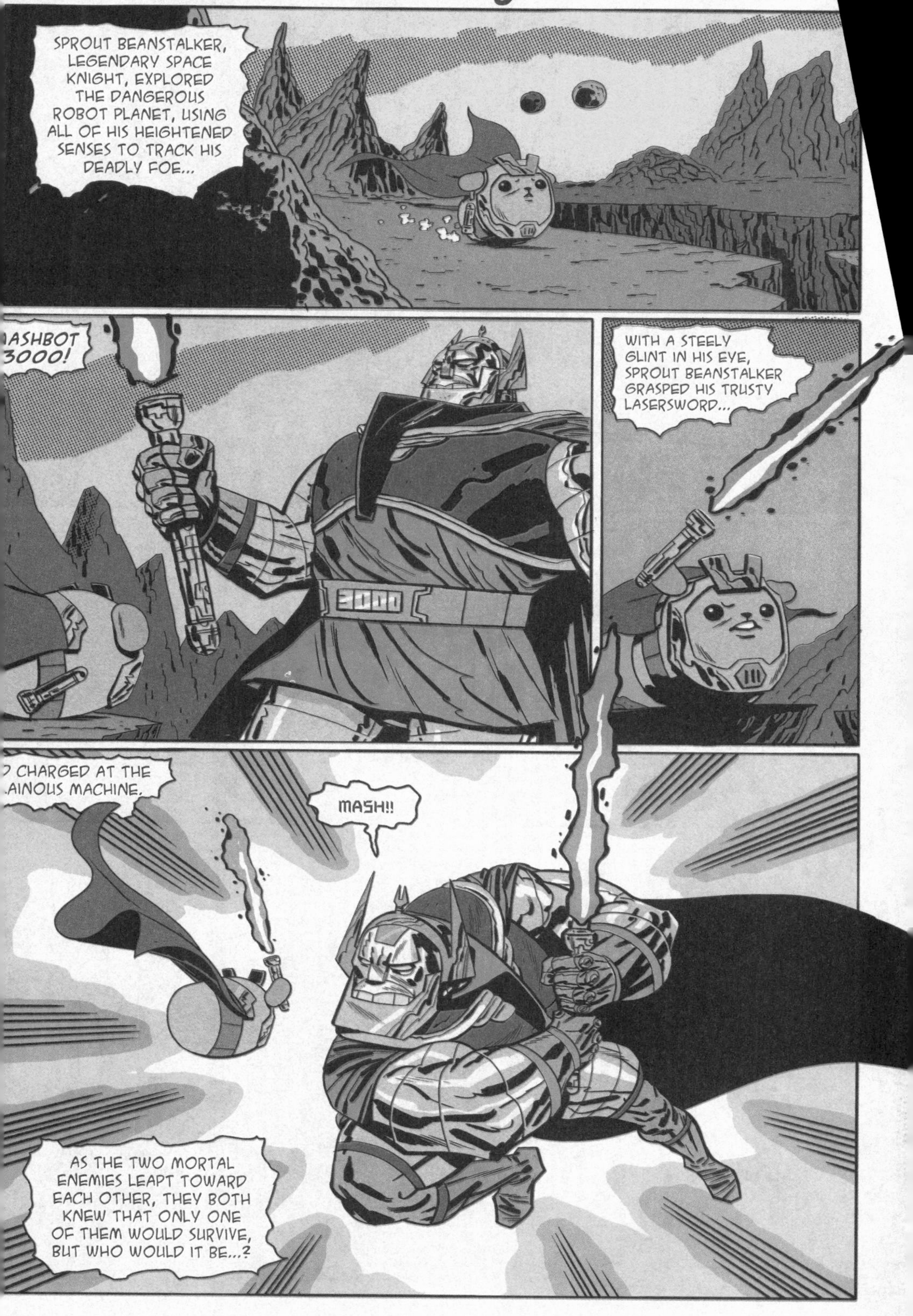
SPROUT BEANSTALKER, LEGENDARY SPACE KNIGHT, EXPLORED THE DANGEROUS ROBOT PLANET, USING ALL OF HIS HEIGHTENED SENSES TO TRACK HIS DEADLY FOE...
ASHBOT 3000!
3000
WITH A STEELY GLINT IN HIS EYE, SPROUT BEANSTALKER GRASPED HIS TRUSTY LASERSWORD...
CHARGED AT THE
AINOUS MACHINE.
MASH!!
AS THE TWO MORTAL ENEMIES LEAPT TOWARD EACH OTHER, THEY BOTH KNEW THAT ONLY ONE OF THEM WOULD SURVIVE, BUT WHO WOULD IT BE...?

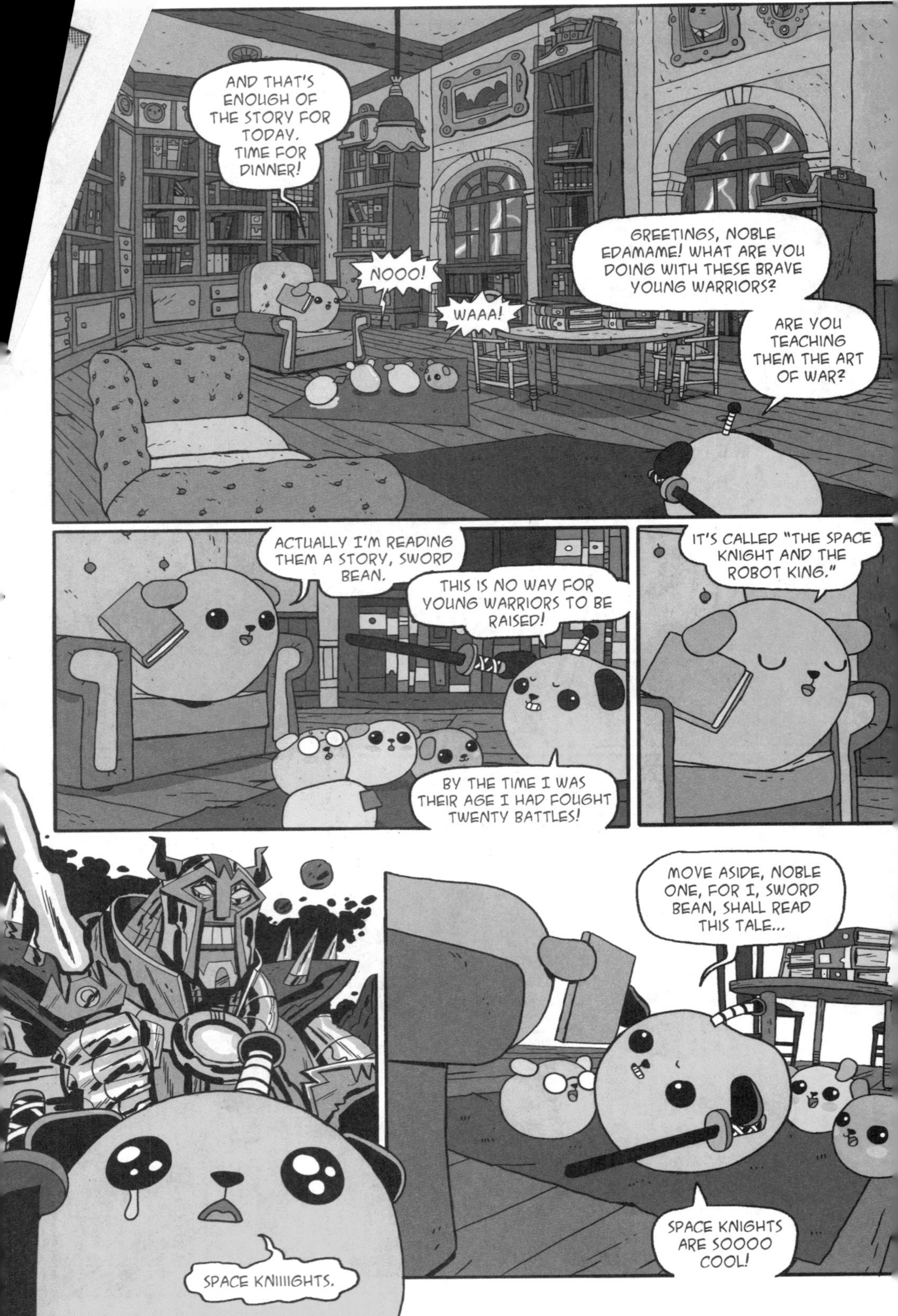
AND THAT'S ENOUGH OF THE STORY FOR TODAY. TIME FOR DINNER!
NOOO!
WAAA!
GREETINGS, NOBLE EDAMAME! WHAT ARE YOU DOING WITH THESE BRAVE YOUNG WARRIORS?
ARE YOU TEACHING THEM THE ART OF WAR?
ACTUALLY I'M READING THEM A STORY, SWORD BEAN.
THIS IS NO WAY FOR YOUNG WARRIORS TO BE RAISED!
BY THE TIME I WAS THEIR AGE I HAD FOUGHT TWENTY BATTLES!
IT'S CALLED "THE SPACE KNIGHT AND THE ROBOT KING."
SPACE KNIIIIGHTS.
MOVE ASIDE, NOBLE ONE, FOR I, SWORD BEAN, SHALL READ THIS TALE...
SPACE KNIGHTS ARE SOOOO COOL!

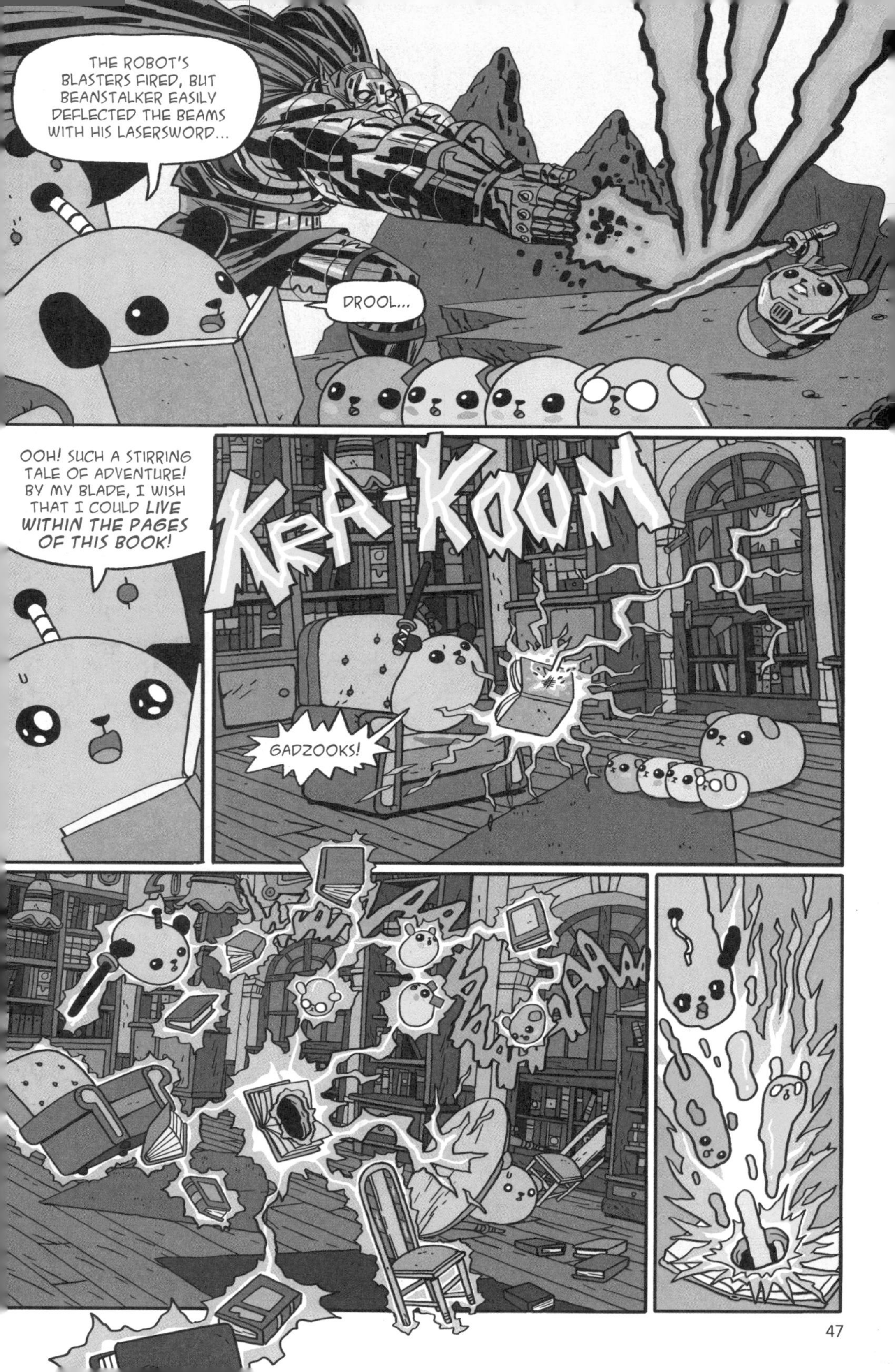
THE ROBOT'S BLASTERS FIRED, BUT BEANSTALKER EASILY DEFLECTED THE BEAMS WITH HIS LASERSWORD...
DROOL...
OOH! SUCH A STIRRING TALE OF ADVENTURE! BY MY BLADE, I WISH THAT I COULD LIVE WITHIN THE PAGES OF THIS BOOK!
KRA-KOOM
GADZOOKS!

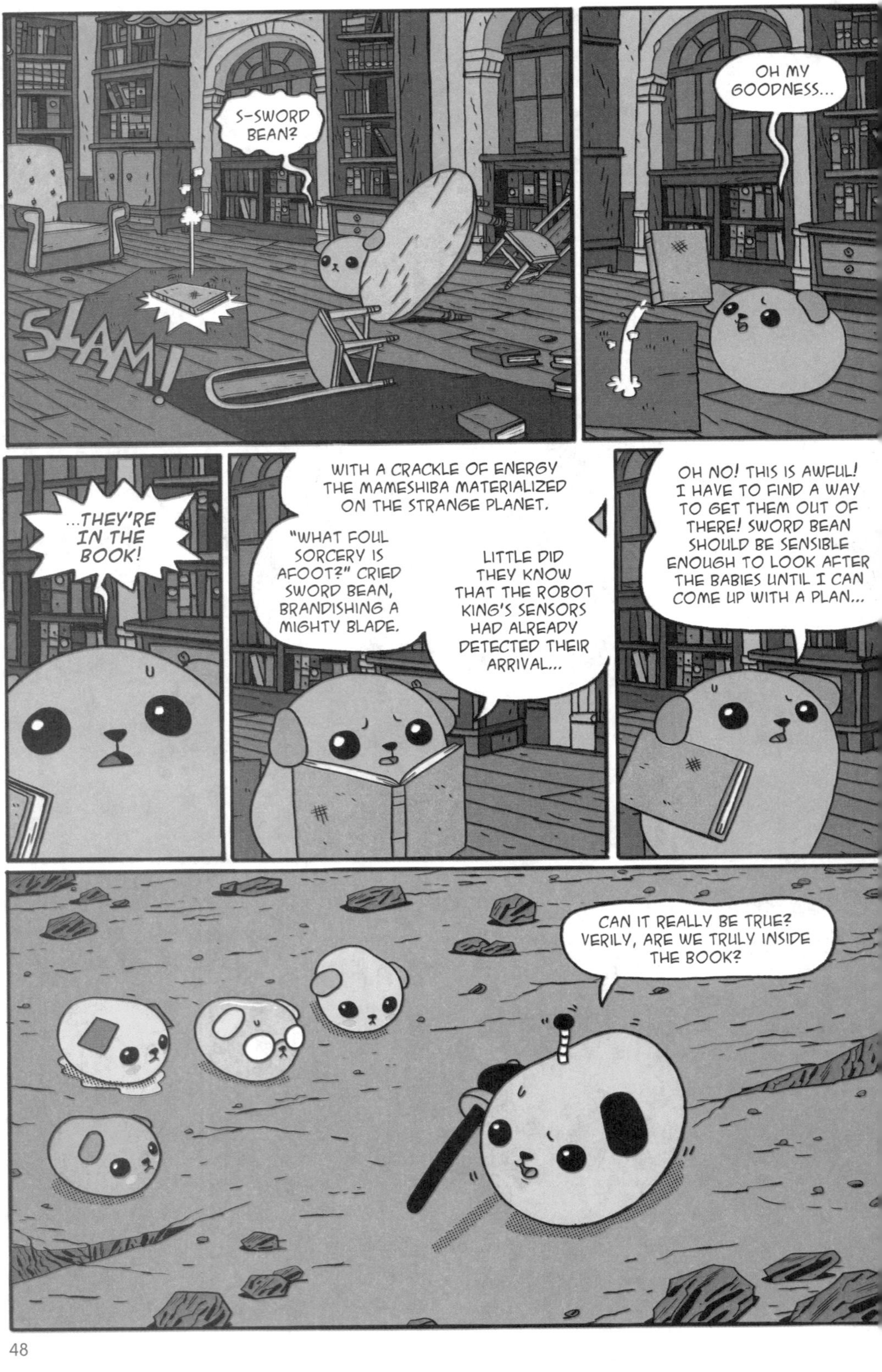
S-SWORD BEAN?
SLAM!
OH MY GOODNESS...
...THEY'RE IN THE BOOK!
WITH A CRACKLE OF ENERGY THE MAMESHIBA MATERIALIZED ON THE STRANGE PLANET.
"WHAT FOUL SORCERY IS AFOOT?" CRIED SWORD BEAN, BRANDISHING A MIGHTY BLADE.
LITTLE DID THEY KNOW THAT THE ROBOT KING'S SENSORS HAD ALREADY DETECTED THEIR ARRIVAL...
OH NO! THIS IS AWFUL! I HAVE TO FIND A WAY TO GET THEM OUT OF THERE! SWORD BEAN SHOULD BE SENSIBLE ENOUGH TO LOOK AFTER THE BABIES UNTIL I CAN COME UP WITH A PLAN...
CAN IT REALLY BE TRUE? VERILY, ARE WE TRULY INSIDE THE BOOK?

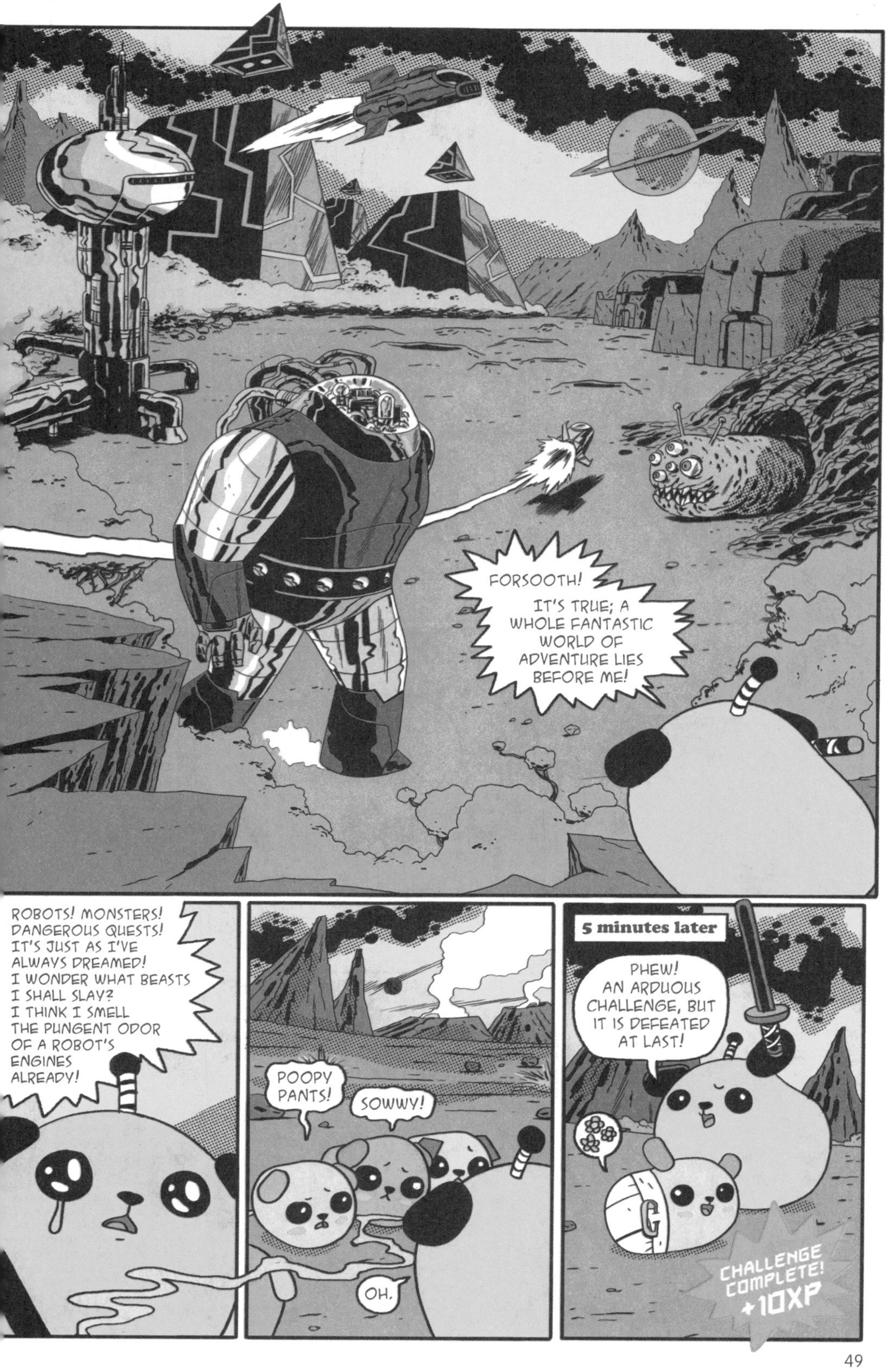
FORSOOTH!
IT'S TRUE; A WHOLE FANTASTIC WORLD OF ADVENTURE LIES BEFORE ME!
ROBOTS! MONSTERS! DANGEROUS QUESTS! IT'S JUST AS I'VE ALWAYS DREAMED! I WONDER WHAT BEASTS I SHALL SLAY? I THINK I SMELL THE PUNGENT ODOR OF A ROBOT'S ENGINES ALREADY!
POOPY PANTS!
SOWWY!
OH.
5 minutes later
PHEW! AN ARDUOUS CHALLENGE, BUT IT IS DEFEATED AT LAST!
CHALLENGE COMPLETE! +10XP

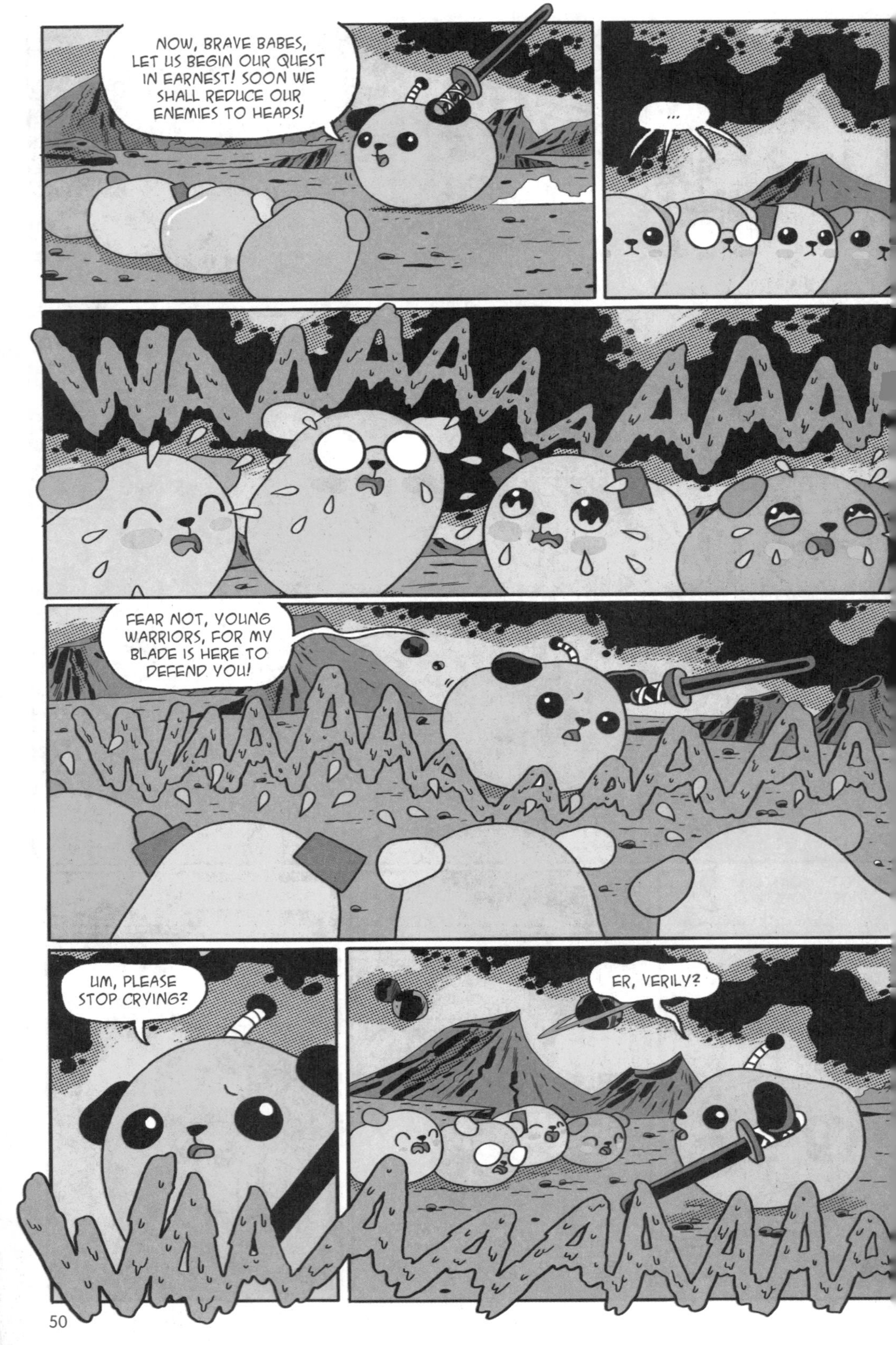
NOW, BRAVE BABES, LET US BEGIN OUR QUEST IN EARNEST! SOON WE SHALL REDUCE OUR ENEMIES TO HEAPS!
...
WAAAAAAAAAA
FEAR NOT, YOUNG WARRIORS, FOR MY BLADE IS HERE TO DEFEND YOU!
WAAAAAAAAAAAAA
UM, PLEASE STOP CRYING?
ER, VERILY?
WAAAAAAAAAA

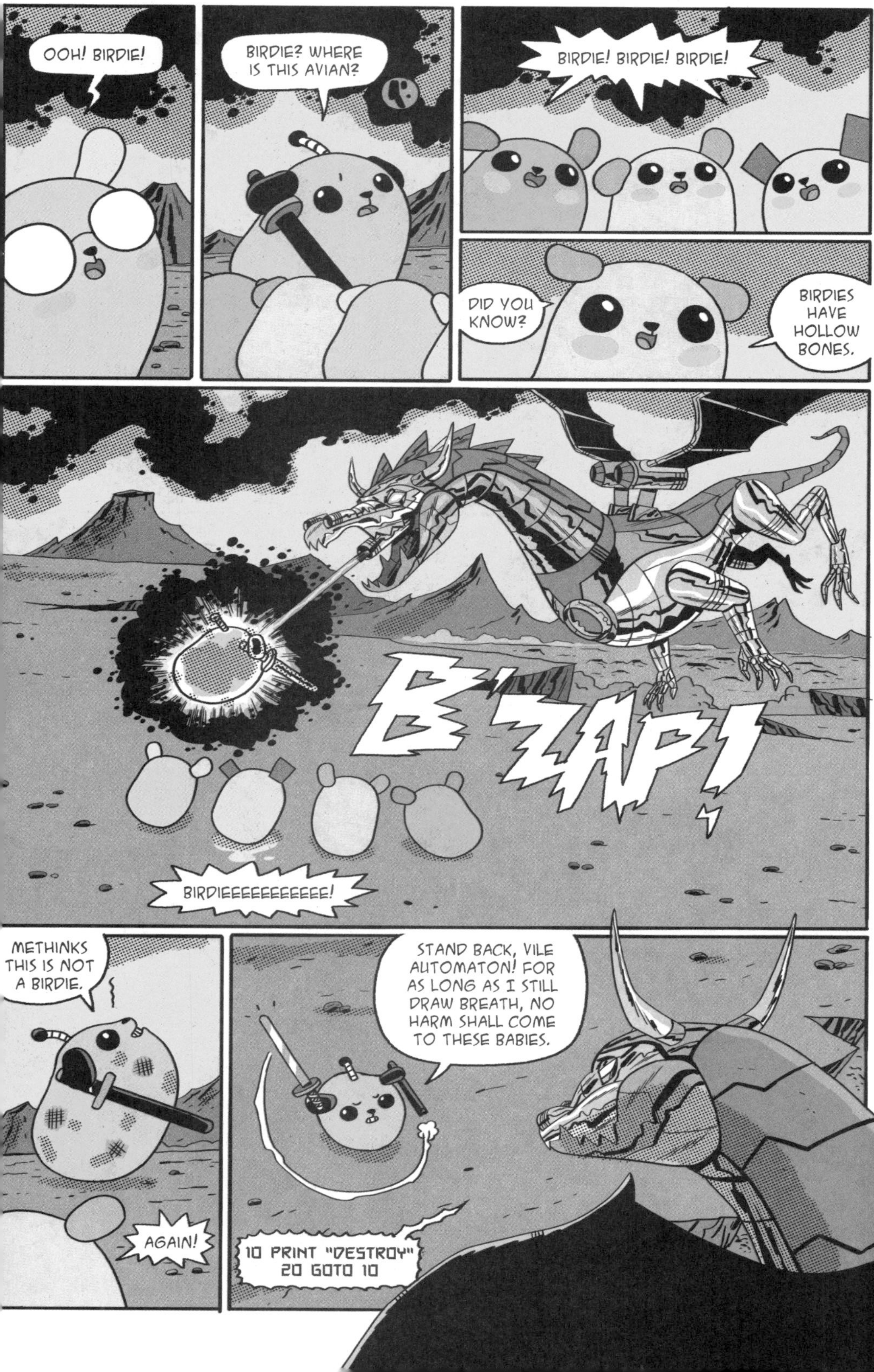
OOH! BIRDIE!
BIRDIE? WHERE IS THIS AVIAN?
BIRDIE! BIRDIE! BIRDIE!
DID YOU KNOW?
BIRDIES HAVE HOLLOW BONES.
B'ZAP!
BIRDIEEEEEEEEEEEEE!
METHINKS THIS IS NOT A BIRDIE.
AGAIN!
STAND BACK, VILE AUTOMATON! FOR AS LONG AS I STILL DRAW BREATH, NO HARM SHALL COME TO THESE BABIES.
10 PRINT "DESTROY"
20 GOTO 10

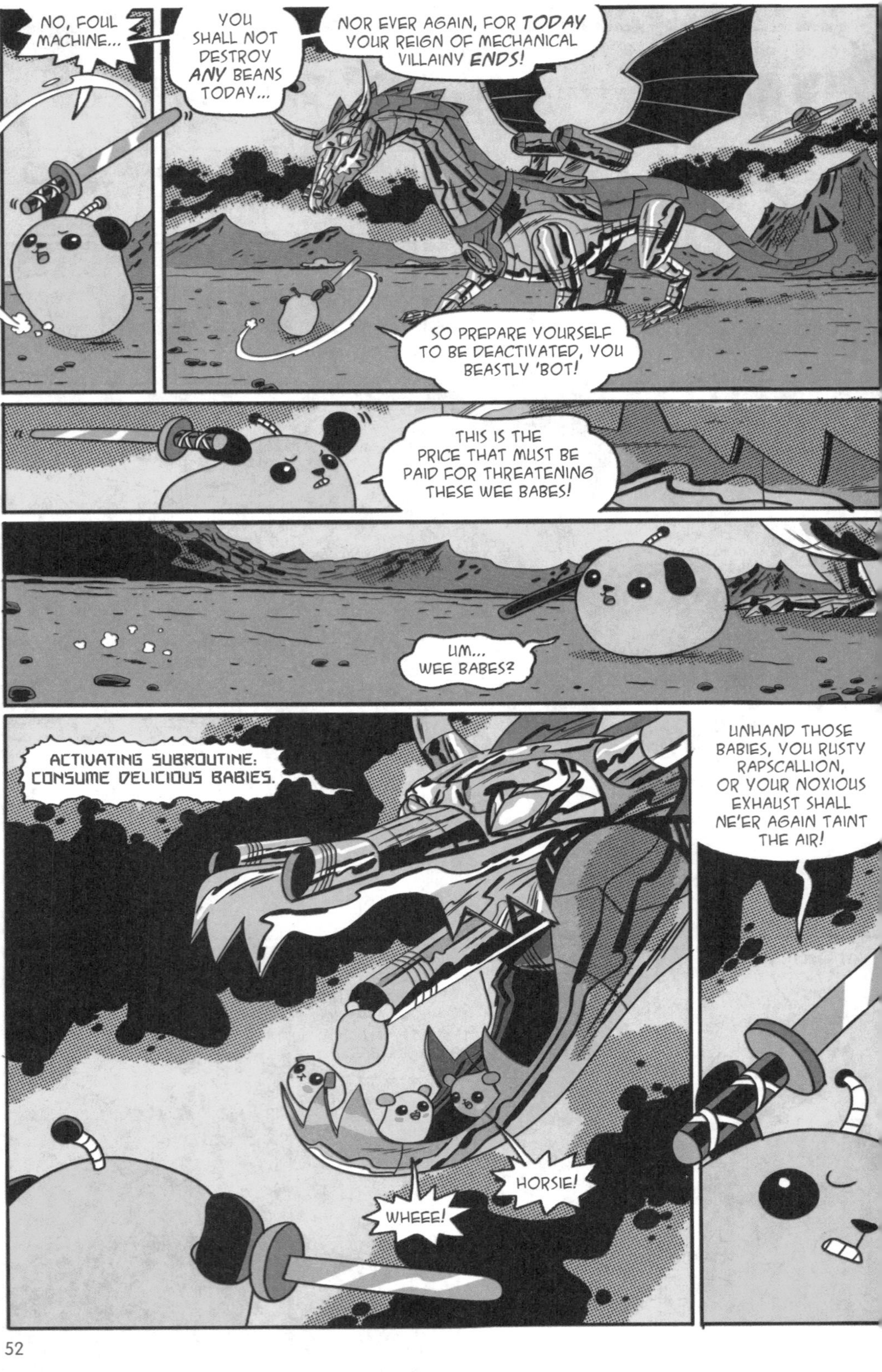
NO, FOUL MACHINE...
YOU SHALL NOT DESTROY ANY BEANS TODAY...
NOR EVER AGAIN, FOR TODAY YOUR REIGN OF MECHANICAL VILLAINY ENDS!
SO PREPARE YOURSELF TO BE DEACTIVATED, YOU BEASTLY 'BOT!
THIS IS THE PRICE THAT MUST BE PAID FOR THREATENING THESE WEE BABES!
UM... WEE BABES?
ACTIVATING SUBROUTINE: CONSUME DELICIOUS BABIES.
UNHAND THOSE BABIES, YOU RUSTY RAPSCALLION, OR YOUR NOXIOUS EXHAUST SHALL NE'ER AGAIN TAINT THE AIR!
HORSIE!
WHEEE!

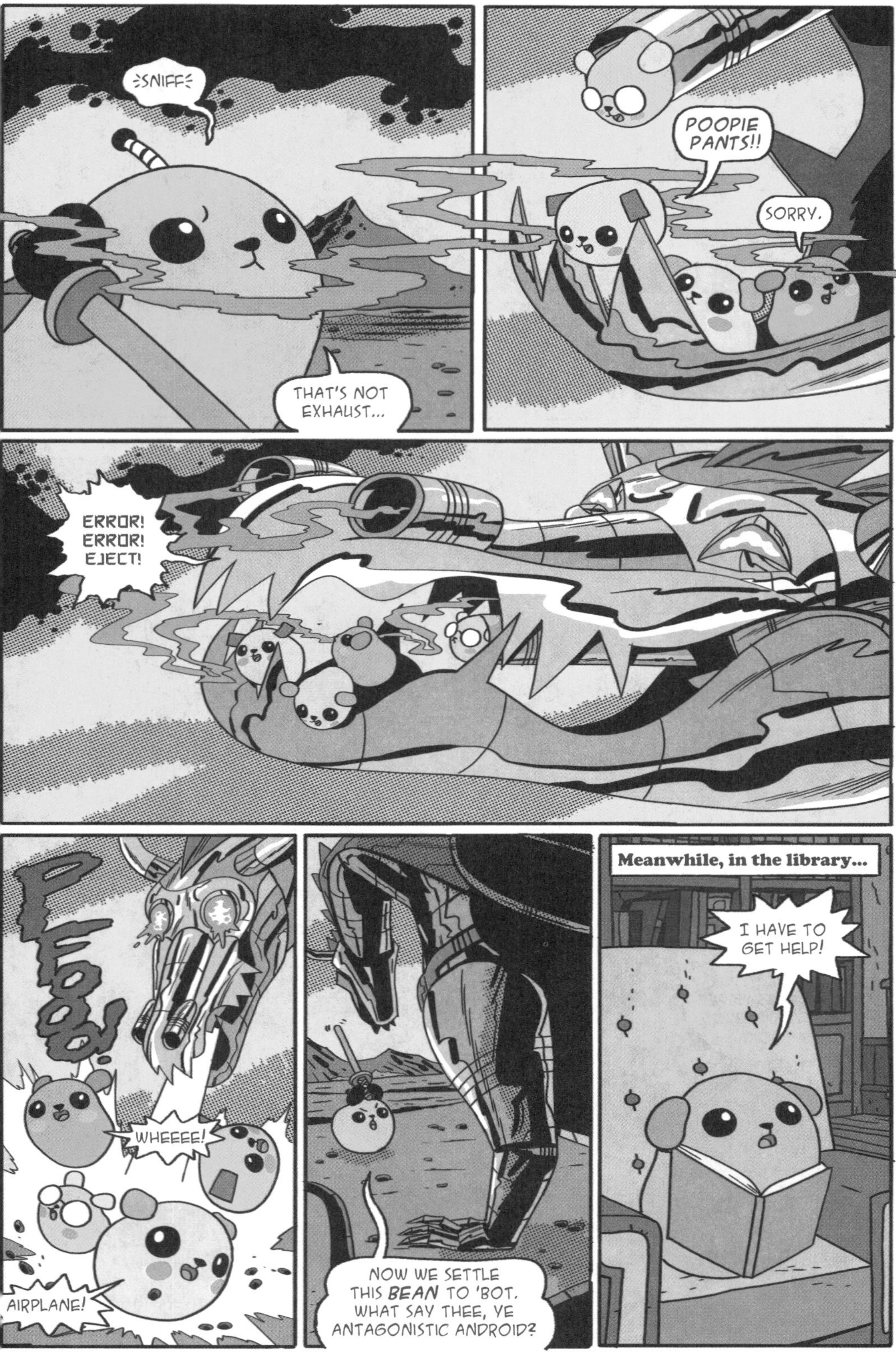
SNIFF
THAT'S NOT EXHAUST...
POOPIE PANTS!!
SORRY.
ERROR! ERROR! EJECT!
PTOOO
WHEEEE!
AIRPLANE!
NOW WE SETTLE THIS BEAN TO 'BOT. WHAT SAY THEE, YE ANTAGONISTIC ANDROID?
Meanwhile, in the library...
I HAVE TO GET HELP!

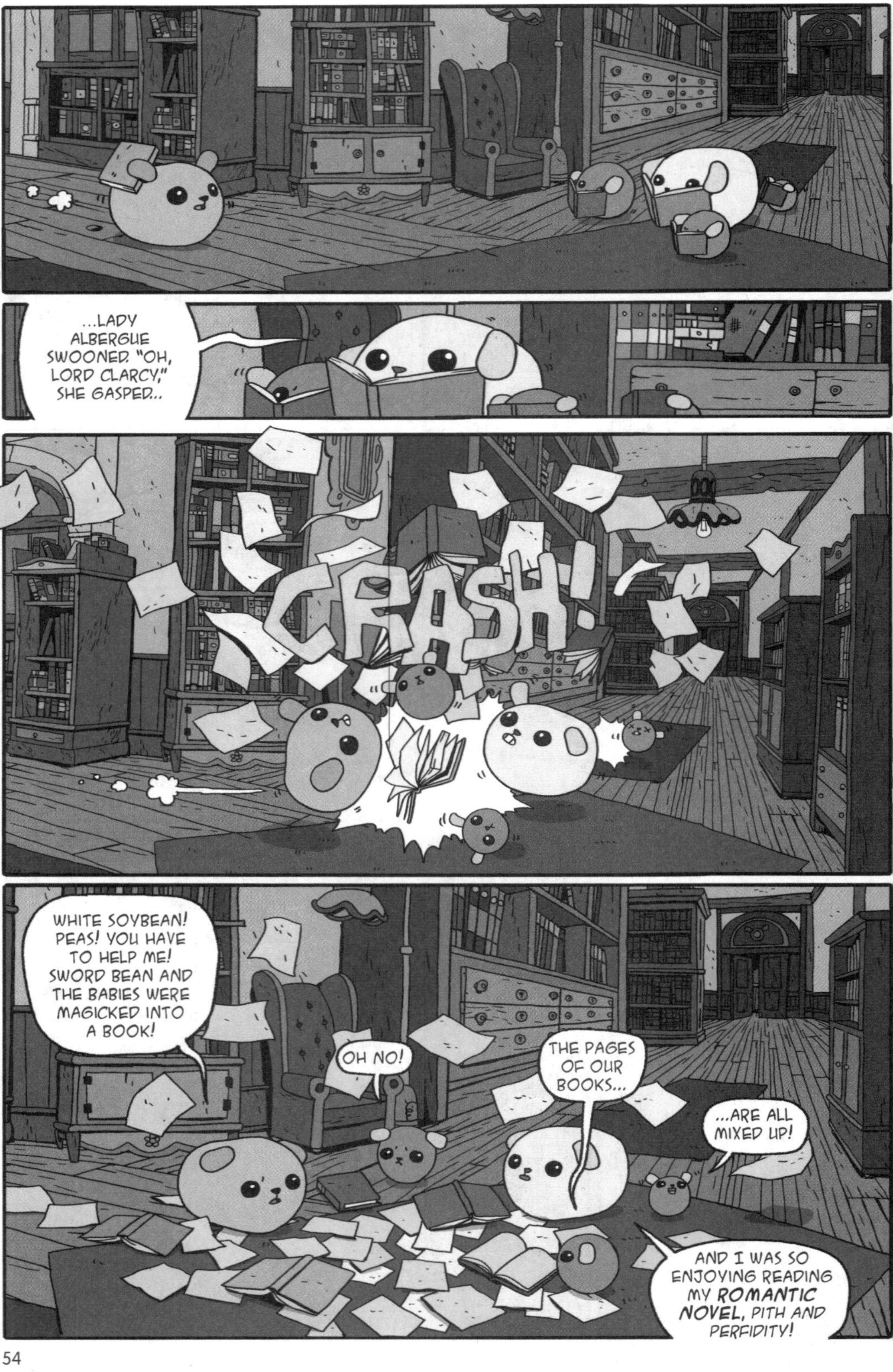

...LADY ALBERGUE SWOONED. "OH, LORD CLARCY," SHE GASPED...
CRASH!
WHITE SOYBEAN! PEAS! YOU HAVE TO HELP ME! SWORD BEAN AND THE BABIES WERE MAGICKED INTO A BOOK!
OH NO!
THE PAGES OF OUR BOOKS...
...ARE ALL MIXED UP!
AND I WAS SO ENJOYING READING MY ROMANTIC NOVEL, PITH AND PERFIDITY!

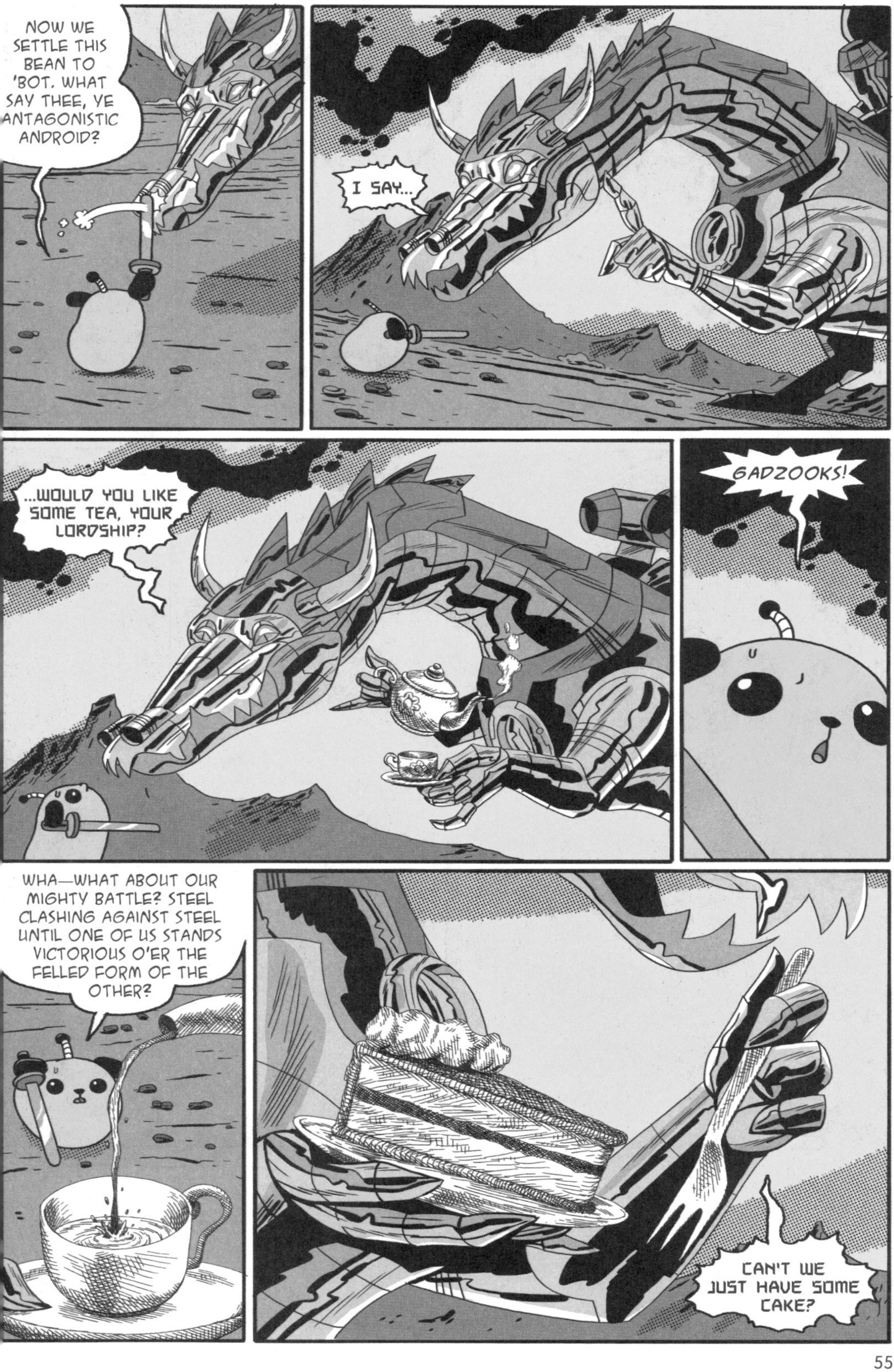
NOW WE SETTLE THIS BEAN TO 'BOT. WHAT SAY THEE, YE ANTAGONISTIC ANDROID?
I SAY...
...WOULD YOU LIKE SOME TEA, YOUR LORDSHIP?
GADZOOKS!
WHA—WHAT ABOUT OUR MIGHTY BATTLE? STEEL CLASHING AGAINST STEEL UNTIL ONE OF US STANDS VICTORIOUS O'ER THE FELLED FORM OF THE OTHER?
CAN'T WE JUST HAVE SOME CAKE?

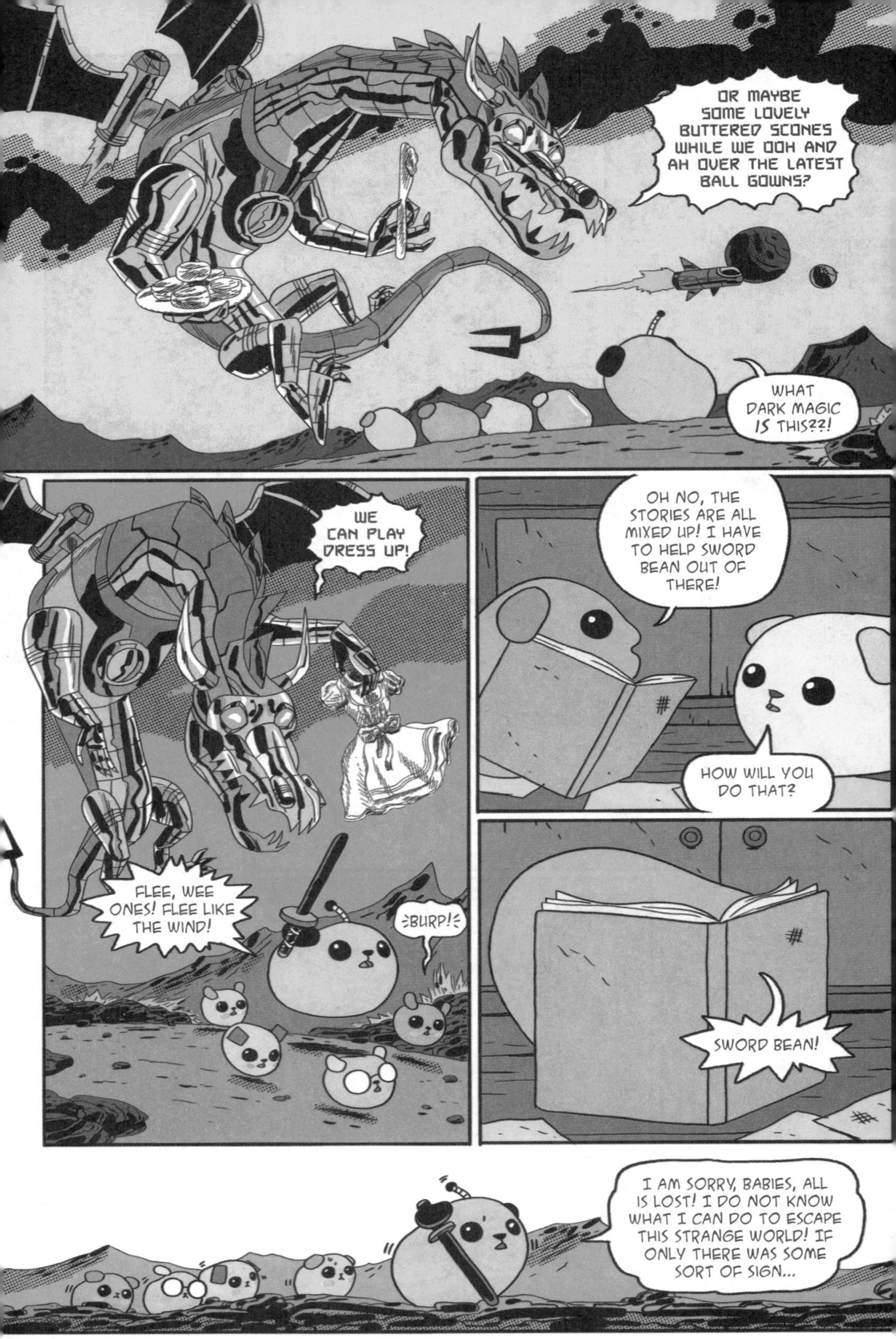
OR MAYBE SOME LOVELY BUTTERED SCONES WHILE WE OOH AND AH OVER THE LATEST BALL GOWNS?
WHAT DARK MAGIC IS THIS??!
WE CAN PLAY DRESS UP!
FLEE, WEE ONES! FLEE LIKE THE WIND!
BURP!
OH NO, THE STORIES ARE ALL MIXED UP! I HAVE TO HELP SWORD BEAN OUT OF THERE!
HOW WILL YOU DO THAT?
SWORD BEAN!
I AM SORRY, BABIES, ALL IS LOST! I DO NOT KNOW WHAT I CAN DO TO ESCAPE THIS STRANGE WORLD! IF ONLY THERE WAS SOME SORT OF SIGN...

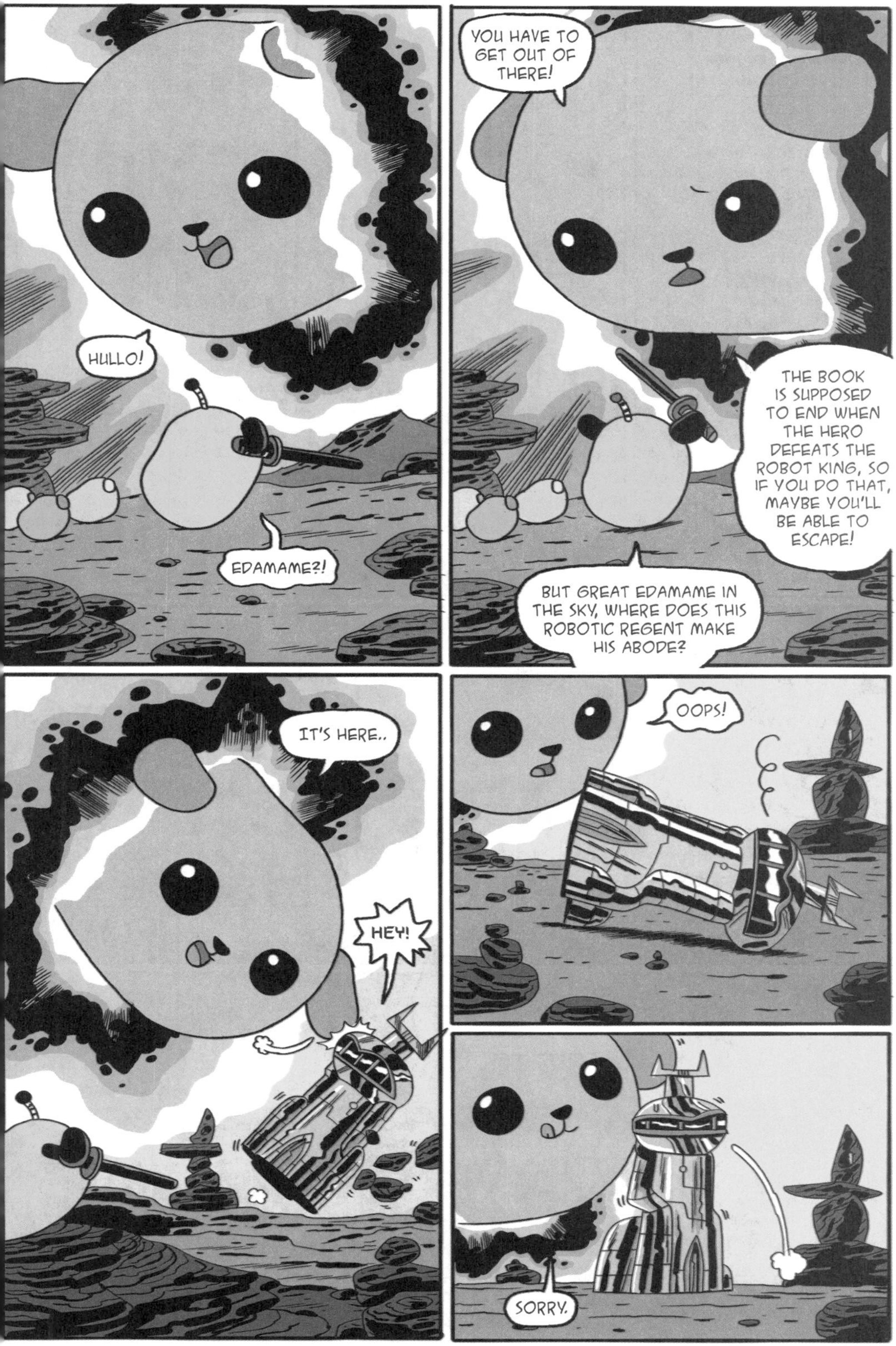
HULLO!
EDAMAME?!
YOU HAVE TO GET OUT OF THERE!
THE BOOK IS SUPPOSED TO END WHEN THE HERO DEFEATS THE ROBOT KING, SO IF YOU DO THAT, MAYBE YOU'LL BE ABLE TO ESCAPE!
BUT GREAT EDAMAME IN THE SKY, WHERE DOES THIS ROBOTIC REGENT MAKE HIS ABODE?
IT'S HERE..
HEY!
OOPS!
SORRY.

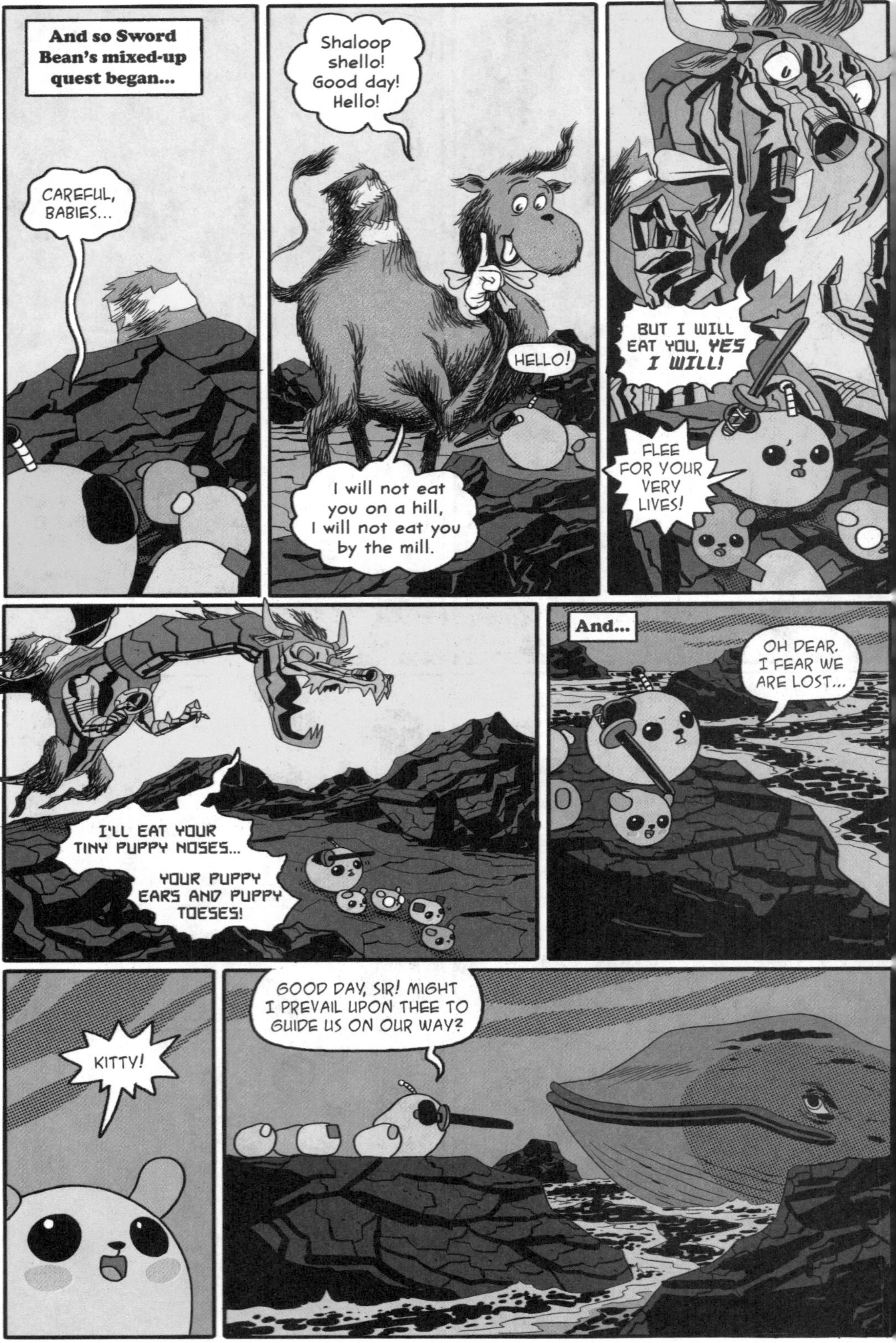

And so Sword Bean's mixed-up quest began...
CAREFUL, BABIES...
Shaloop shello! Good day! Hello!
HELLO!
I will not eat you on a hill, I will not eat you by the mill.
BUT I WILL EAT YOU, YES I WILL!
FLEE FOR YOUR VERY LIVES!
I'LL EAT YOUR TINY PUPPY NOSES...
YOUR PUPPY EARS AND PUPPY TOESES!
And...
OH DEAR. I FEAR WE ARE LOST...
KITTY!
GOOD DAY, SIR! MIGHT I PREVAIL UPON THEE TO GUIDE US ON OUR WAY?

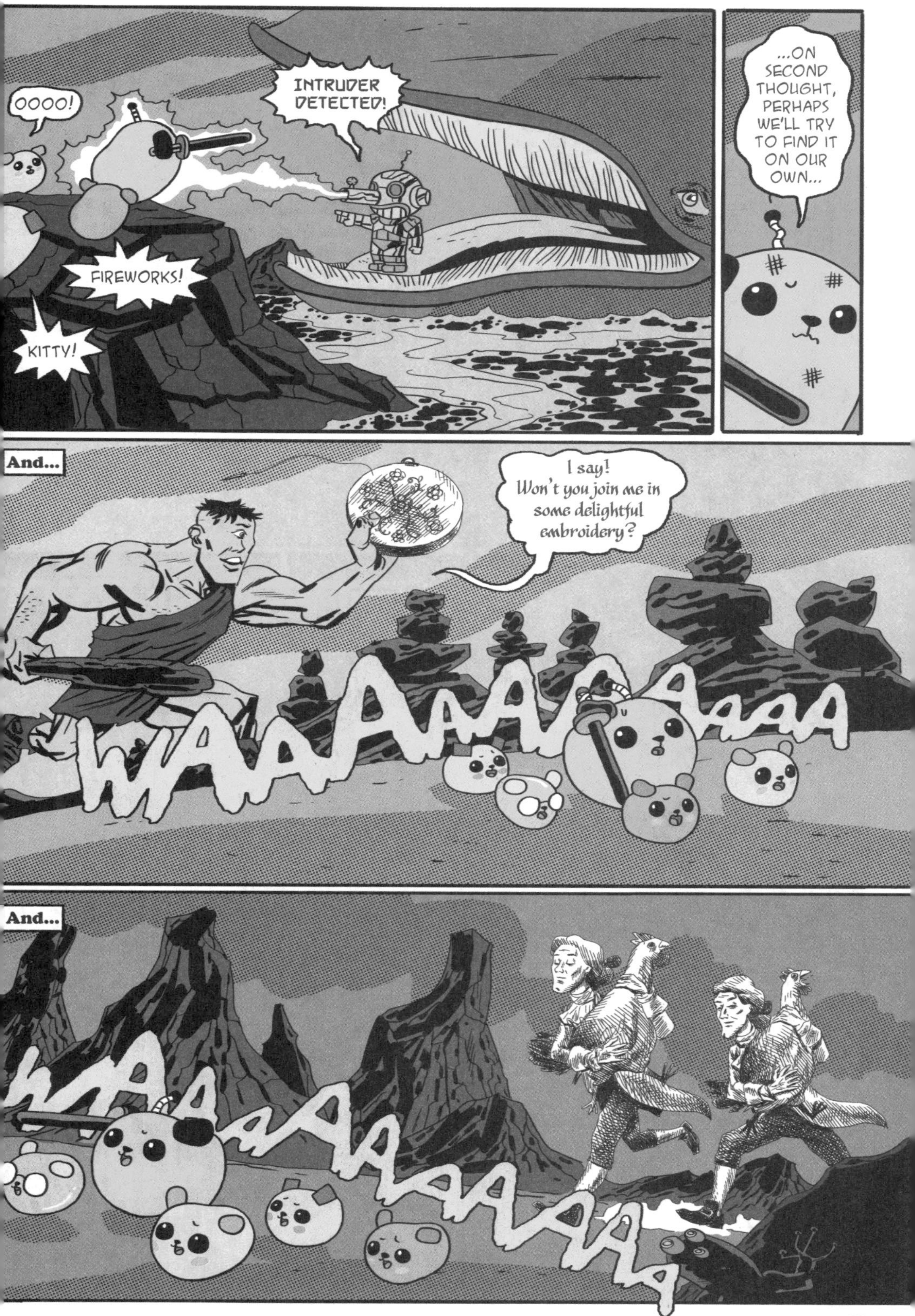
OOOO!
INTRUDER DETECTED!
FIREWORKS!
KITTY!
...ON SECOND THOUGHT, PERHAPS WE'LL TRY TO FIND IT ON OUR OWN...
And...
I say! Won't you join me in some delightful embroidery?
WAAAAAAAaaaa
And...
WAAAAAAAAAAAAAA

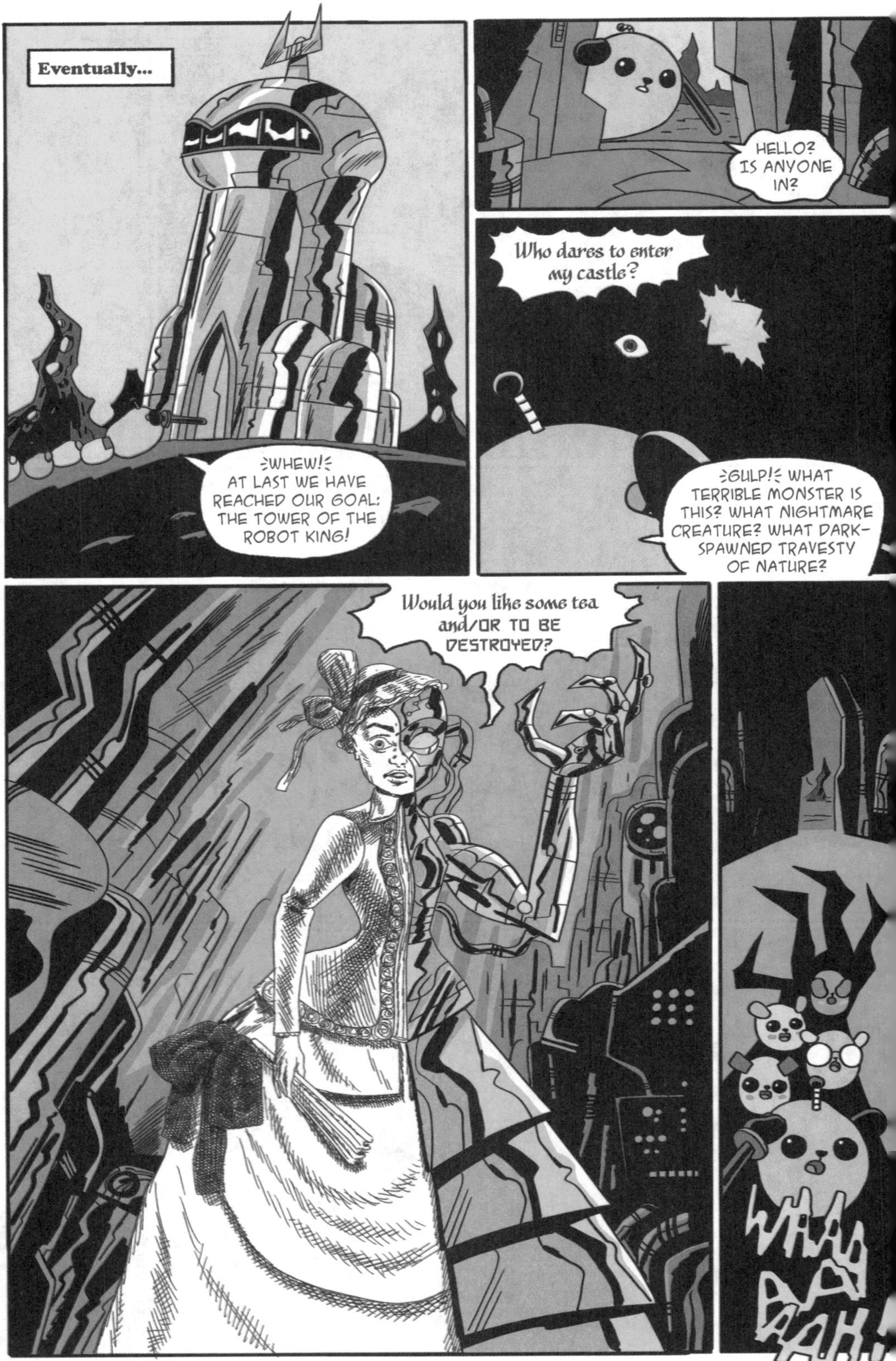
Eventually...
≡WHEW!≡ AT LAST WE HAVE REACHED OUR GOAL: THE TOWER OF THE ROBOT KING!
HELLO? IS ANYONE IN?
Who dares to enter my castle?
≡GULP!≡ WHAT TERRIBLE MONSTER IS THIS? WHAT NIGHTMARE CREATURE? WHAT DARK-SPAWNED TRAVESTY OF NATURE?
Would you like some tea and/OR TO BE DESTROYED?
WHAAAAAH!

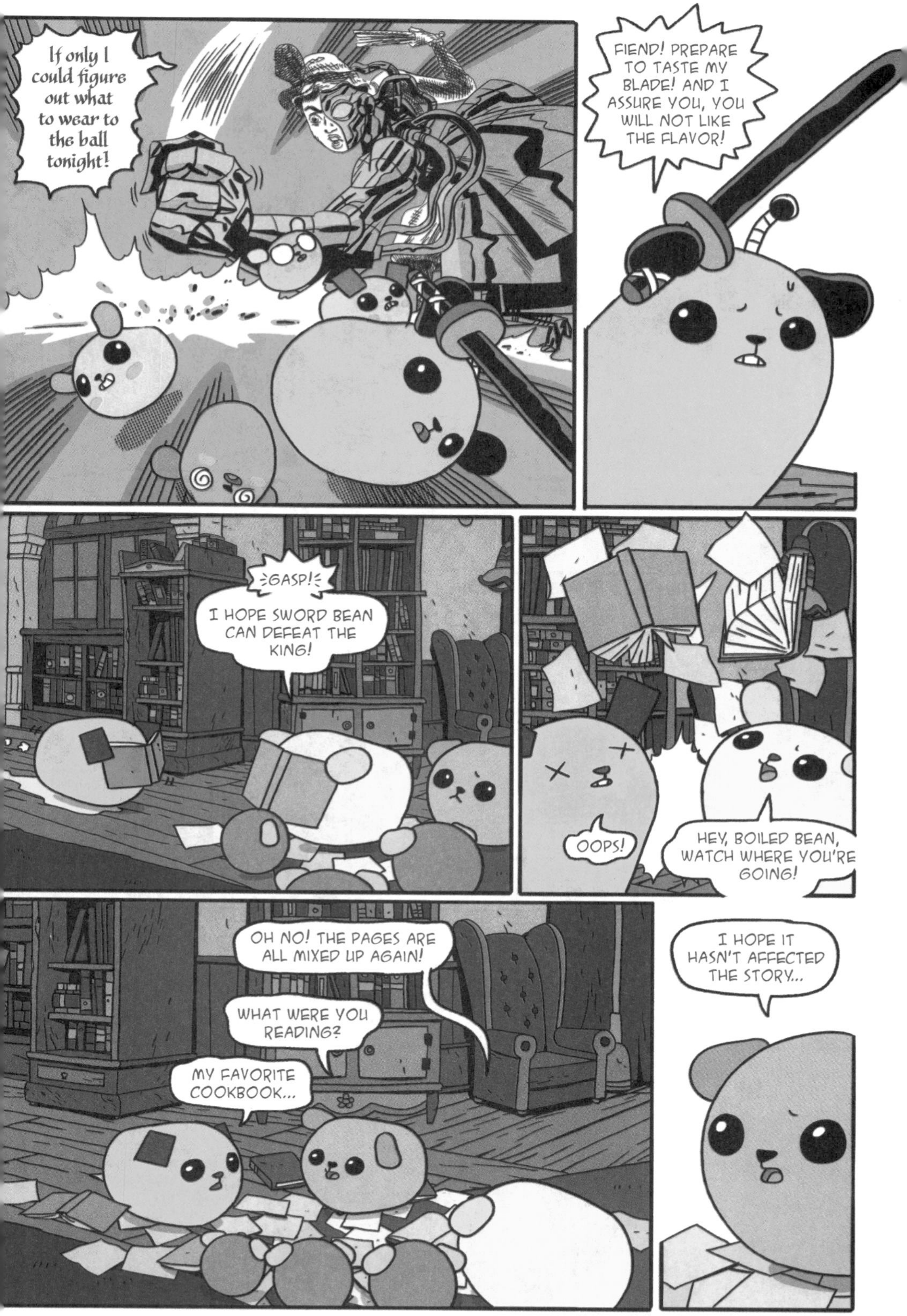
If only I could figure out what to wear to the ball tonight!
FIEND! PREPARE TO TASTE MY BLADE! AND I ASSURE YOU, YOU WILL NOT LIKE THE FLAVOR!
GASP!
I HOPE SWORD BEAN CAN DEFEAT THE KING!
OOPS!
HEY, BOILED BEAN, WATCH WHERE YOU'RE GOING!
OH NO! THE PAGES ARE ALL MIXED UP AGAIN!
WHAT WERE YOU READING?
MY FAVORITE COOKBOOK...
I HOPE IT HASN'T AFFECTED THE STORY...

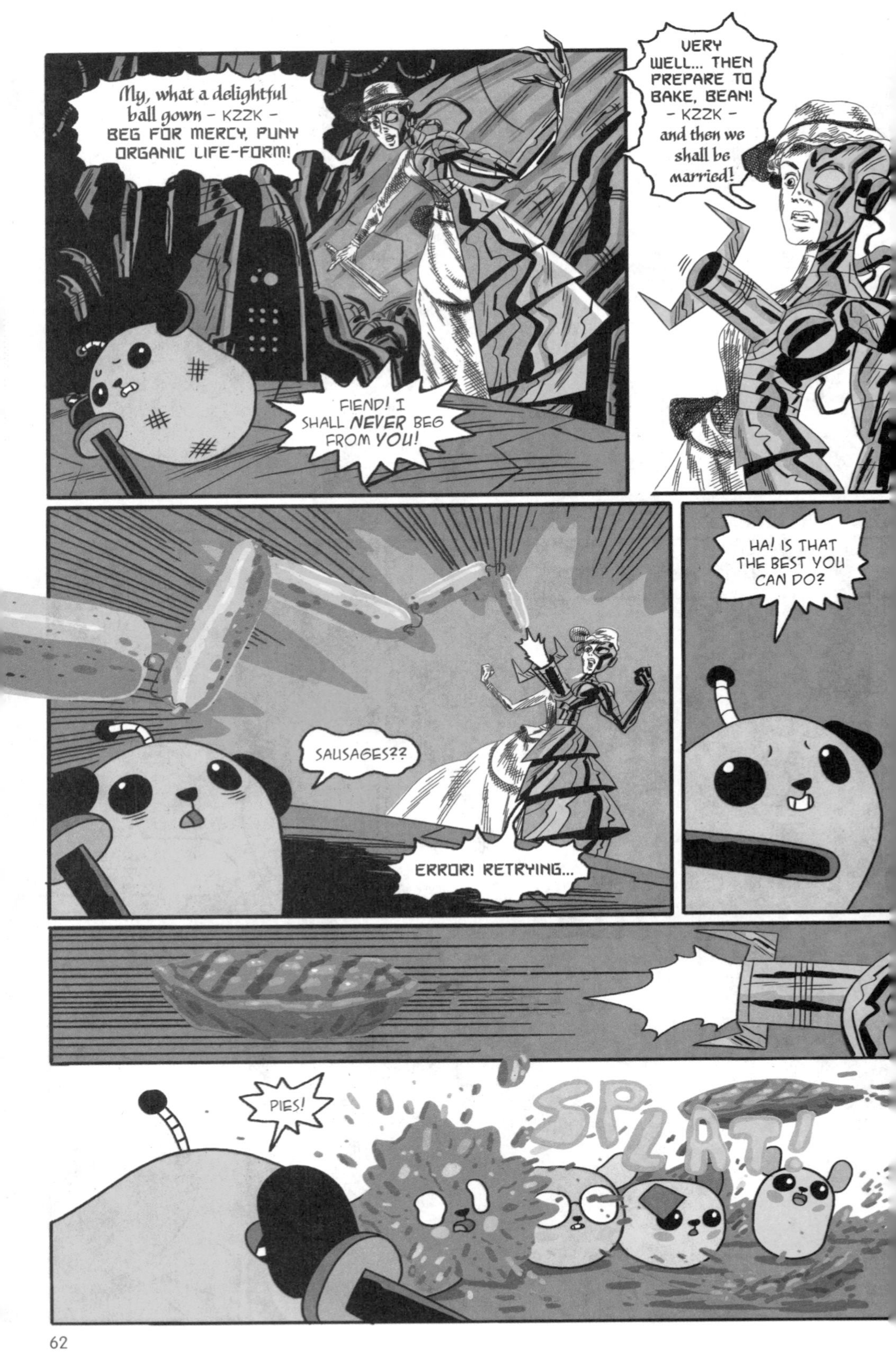
My, what a delightful ball gown - KZZK - BEG FOR MERCY, PUNY ORGANIC LIFE-FORM!
VERY WELL... THEN PREPARE TO BAKE, BEAN! - KZZK - and then we shall be married!
FIEND! I SHALL NEVER BEG FROM YOU!
SAUSAGES??
ERROR! RETRYING...
HA! IS THAT THE BEST YOU CAN DO?
PIES!
SPLAT!

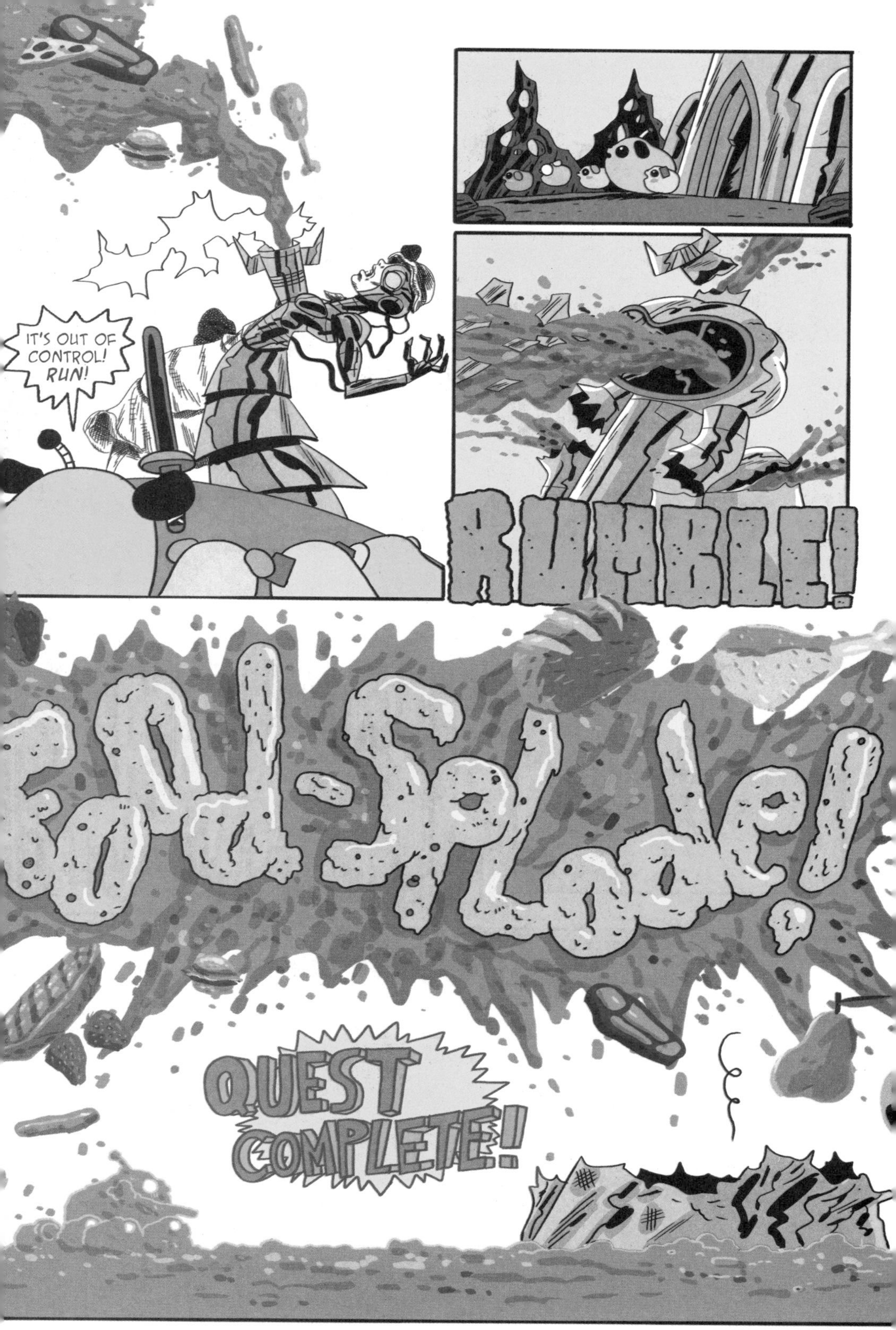
IT'S OUT OF CONTROL! RUN!
RUMBLE!
FOOD-SPLODE!
QUEST COMPLETE!

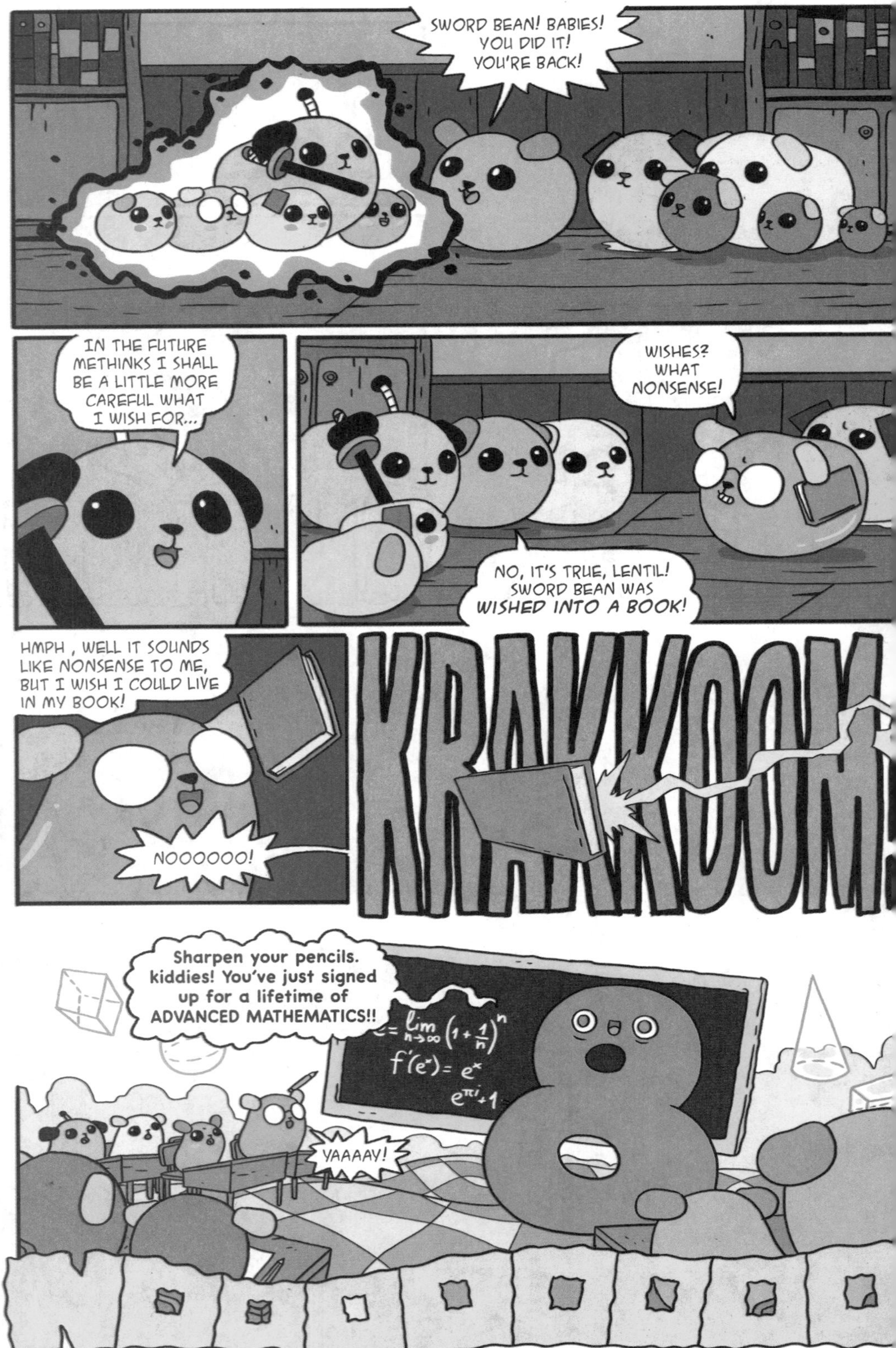
SWORD BEAN! BABIES! YOU DID IT! YOU'RE BACK!
IN THE FUTURE METHINKS I SHALL BE A LITTLE MORE CAREFUL WHAT I WISH FOR...
WISHES? WHAT NONSENSE!
NO, IT'S TRUE, LENTIL! SWORD BEAN WAS WISHED INTO A BOOK!
HMPH, WELL IT SOUNDS LIKE NONSENSE TO ME, BUT I WISH I COULD LIVE IN MY BOOK!
KRAKKOOM
NOOOOOO!
Sharpen your pencils. kiddies! You've just signed up for a lifetime of ADVANCED MATHEMATICS!!
YAAAAY!
NO
The En